HEALING GABRIEL

ELIZABETH KELLY

EK PUBLISHING INC.

HEALING GABRIEL

Will her love heal his wounds?

Fifteen years ago, Gabriel Dern was involved in a car accident that left terrible scars covering half of his body. He retreats from society and rejects the idea of ever finding a woman who will accept him for who he is.

After her mother's death, Morgan Wilson moves to the small town of Martinvale to begin her new life. While living in the carriage house on Gabriel's property, she gradually tears down the walls Gabe has built around him.

As Gabe slowly warms up to her, Morgan must find a way to convince him she wants both his friendship and his love.

CHAPTER 1

"**M**s. Wilson!"

Morgan finished wiping the white board and turned to see the little girl barreling towards her. Her mother trailed behind her.

"Hi, Natalia." Morgan knelt and hugged the blonde-haired girl. "What are you still doing here?"

"Mama wants to talk to you."

"Hi, Morgan." Natalia's mother smiled and leaned against the corner of Morgan's desk.

"Hi, Lacey. How are you?"

"Good." She watched as Natalia wandered to her desk and opened the lid before rummaging through it.

"So, what's up?" Morgan tripped over the leg of her desk and fell into her chair.

"You okay?"

"Fine." She rubbed her knee where she had banged it against the seat of her chair. "I'm just clumsy."

"You really are," Lacey laughed. "I've never seen anyone as uncoordinated as you. You must be one giant walking bruise."

Morgan grinned. "You should see the one I have on my side right now."

Lacey patted her arm. "Would you like to join us this weekend for a barbeque? Peter's got grilling fever."

"I'd love to. Thanks for the invite. That's really nice of you."

Lacey shrugged. "I figured it would be a good way for you to meet some more people. This is a small town, and it can be hard to meet other single people."

Morgan gave her a wary look. "Are you trying to set me up with someone?"

Lacey laughed. "No, I swear I'm not. But I thought you might like to meet other people who can go out on a Friday night at a moment's notice."

Morgan eyed her suspiciously. She had moved to town two months ago and started her new job as the grade one teacher at Martinvale Elementary. Natalia was one of her students, and Morgan and Lacey quickly hit it off at the parent/teacher meet and greet.

She was thankful for Lacey's friendship. She moved to Martinvale after leaving the city she had called home for over fifteen years. After her mother died, she'd grown restless and tired of the city and her teaching position at one of the private schools. She applied for the job in Martinvale on a whim and was shocked when she was offered the position.

The following three months had been a whirlwind of selling her mother's home, sorting her possessions, and saying goodbye to her friends, coworkers, and students. Spurred by the urge for a clean start, she sold most of her mother's furniture and put most of her personal items into storage before moving to Martinvale.

"I promise I'm not," Lacey repeated. She sat on the corner of the desk and examined her brightly-painted fingernails. "How's the house hunt going?"

Morgan loaded her laptop into the pink computer bag. "Not great. I'm tired of living out of that motel. Although," she brightened, "I'm looking at a townhouse on Denver Street next week. It looked promising."

Lacey winced. "Yeah, don't bother."

"What? Why not?"

"Denver Street is in an awful part of town, Morgan. Just trust me – you don't want to live there. Not unless you like having drug deals going down outside your front door."

Morgan sighed. "This is ridiculous. Who knew it would be so difficult to find a place to live here? Maybe I'm just too picky."

Lacey hesitated. "I might know of a place."

"Really?"

"Yeah. It's a little bit outside of town, but as long as you don't mind a longer drive to work…"

"I don't care," Morgan said eagerly. "Tell me about it."

"It's my parents' farm. After they died, my brother took over. He works from home, and he raises sheep as a hobby."

Morgan frowned. "I didn't know you had a brother." She had gone for coffee and been to Lacey and Peter's place half a dozen times, and Lacey had never mentioned a brother.

"He keeps to himself. Anyway, there's the main farmhouse and a small carriage house behind it. Peter and I lived in it for a while after we first got married. It's small but cozy. I'm sure my brother will rent it to you until you find the perfect place to buy."

"Lacey, I can't thank you enough." Morgan hugged the small blonde woman impulsively. "I am so sick of living out of a motel."

Lacey returned her hug. "You're welcome. Why don't we meet there tomorrow night around seven? I'll text you the address."

* * *

MORGAN STEPPED OUT OF HER CAR AND GLANCED AROUND curiously. A large blue truck was parked in the driveway, but no sign of Lacey's car. She leaned against her vehicle momentarily, then walked towards the large white farmhouse. She would introduce herself to Lacey's brother while she waited for Lacey.

She knocked on the front door of the farmhouse and waited patiently. After a few moments, she knocked again. When there was still no answer, she stepped off the porch and walked around the side of the house, gasping in delight. The backyard was a gorgeous jungle of flowers. It was early spring, but there were already lots of bright blooms of flowers nodding in the slight breeze. She could only imagine how beautiful it would be in the summer.

She could see the carriage house at the back of the yard, and she followed the small footpath of stones, stopping to smell a fragrant bright yellow hyacinth bush. She climbed the small porch, tripping on the stairs but catching herself before she could fall, and peered into one of the front windows. She cupped her hands around her face to cut the setting sun's glare.

She knocked on the door and tried the handle when there was no answer. It turned easily under her hand, and she entered the cool, slightly musty-smelling house. She was standing in the kitchen, and she squinted in the gloom and tried the light switch. Nothing happened, and she shrugged and moved deeper into the house.

It could use a good cleaning, but she was immediately charmed by the small house. She walked down the hallway, peeking through the first doorway to see the small living room. Furniture, covered in dusty white sheets, filled the room, and she continued down the hall. A door on the left opened to reveal a small bathroom. She grinned delightedly at the old-fashioned bath tub and ran her hand over the pedestal sink before returning to the hallway. There was a door at the end, and she opened it, expecting to see a small bedroom. It was a bedroom, but it was much larger than she'd anticipated. A gas fireplace was on the far wall with a small sitting area, and a double bed, hidden under a large sheet, was pushed up against the wall next to it.

It would be so nice to lay in bed on a cold night and read with the fireplace going. Already half in love with the place, she moved toward the large window, intending to pull back the dark curtains to see the room more clearly.

As she reached for the curtains, a low growling started behind her. She turned and stared at the dog standing in the doorway. It was an Australian shepherd type dog, she imagined Lacey's brother probably used it to help herd the sheep, and she stared steadily at it.

She wasn't afraid of dogs, not even ones that were growling at her, and she said, "Good dog," in a calm and confident voice.

The dog stopped growling and cocked his head at her.

"Come here, puppy." She made a kissing noise and patted her leg. The dog slunk into the room, its tail between its legs and nose sniffing the air delicately.

She made another kissing noise and waited patiently as the dog drew closer. It sniffed at her pant leg, and she said, "Good dog," but made no move to pet it. It sniffed at her hand, and when its tail wagged, she patted its neck.

"Such a good doggie." The dog chuffed and nudged her with its cold nose. She smiled and scratched the deep fur on his neck. "Does that feel good, puppy? Do you want a bum rub? Huh? Does the good puppy want a bum rub?"

She scratched the top of the dog's back near its rump. The dog gave another soft chuff and pressed its upper body against her legs. Its whole back end was wagging now, and she laughed. "Does that feel good? What's your name, puppy? Do you have a collar?"

She searched around the thick fur of its neck and found its collar. A rough voice spoke from the doorway before she could see a name tag. "Who the hell are you?"

She jumped, and the dog gave a short bark and skittered away. Her heart thumping in her chest, she squinted at the shadowy figure standing in the doorway.

"Hi, my name's Morgan. I'm a friend of Lacey's. You must be her brother." She started forward, her hand held out, and the man took another step back.

"Don't come any closer. Why are you here?" He snapped.

The dog weaved anxiously around his legs, whining and staring at him. He rested his hand briefly on the dog's head, and it sat beside him, tail thumping against the floor.

Morgan stopped and stared nervously at the man. She was starting to get a bad feeling in her stomach, and she glanced uneasily around the room. He was blocking her way out, and tingles of alarm raced down her spine.

"Are you not Lacey's brother?"

"I am. Answer my question – why are you here?"

She took a deep breath. "I'm meeting Lacey here. She said I might be able to rent the carriage house from you. I'm new in town. I, um, I teach at the elementary school. Natalia's one of my students."

She was babbling, her nerves getting the best of her, and she suddenly turned and grabbed the curtains. "Do you mind if I open the curtains? It's dark in here."

"No! Wait -"

She ignored him and drew back the curtains, blinking as the light from the setting sun flooded into the room.

"There, that's better." She turned around, and her breath caught in her throat. The man had moved across the bedroom with a silent, spooky speed until he stood directly behind her.

"Did you come to see the freak? Is that it?" He took her arm and pushed her until her back was pressed against the cold glass of the window. "Take a good look then, sweetheart."

The sun highlighted the burn scars on the left side of his face. They started at his temple and swept down his face and neck to disappear inside the collar of his shirt.

His dark blue eyes glittered angrily at her as she stared at the scars on his face. "Satisfied? Get a good enough look? Are you -"

"Gabriel!"

The man turned, and Morgan breathed a sigh of relief when she saw Lacey standing in the bedroom doorway. Natalia was with her, and she hugged the dog before running toward them.

"Hi, Uncle Gabe!" She jumped at him, and he caught her, picking her up and settling her in the crook of his arm.

"Hi, Nat. What are you doing here?"

"We're showing Ms. Wilson the house. Mama says she's going to live here."

Gabe glanced back at Morgan before staring at Lacey. "Did she now? Lacey, can I speak with you in private, please?"

Lacey shook her head. "Nope."

She walked by her brother and daughter, glaring fiercely at Gabriel over Natalia's head before smiling at Morgan. She linked her arm around Morgan's and squeezed.

"Morgan, this is my brother Gabriel Dern. Gabe, this is Natalia's teacher and my friend, Morgan Wilson."

"It's nice to meet you, Mr. Dern." Morgan held out her

ELIZABETH KELLY

hand. Gabriel grunted in reply and took her hand. An unexpected shiver ran through her at his touch, and he immediately pulled his hand away, turning away so that the burned side of his face would be hidden from her view.

"Call him Gabe," Lacey said airily. "So, what do you think of the place, Morgan?"

"It's very nice," Morgan said. "If it's available, I'll take it."

"Actually," Gabe set Natalia down and scowled at Lacey, "it's not for rent. I don't -"

"Be quiet, Gabriel," Lacey said. "It is for rent, and Morgan, we'd be happy to have you stay here."

"Lacey -"

Lacey sighed and touched Natalia's head. "Honey, why don't you show Ms. Wilson the barn while I speak with your Uncle Gabe? I bet she'd like to see it."

"Okay." Natalia held her hand out. "Come on, Ms. Wilson. The barn smells, but there are new kittens in it."

Morgan took her hand, giving Lacey an uncertain look. "Lacey, maybe -"

"Go on, Morgan. I'll be right out." Lacey smiled at her, and Morgan allowed Natalia to take her out of the room.

* * *

GABRIEL FLINCHED WHEN LACEY SMACKED HIM HARD ON HIS arm the second Natalia and Morgan were out of earshot. "What the hell, Gabriel? You're being so rude."

"I'm being rude? I find some chick wandering around my house, and I'm being the rude one? And what the hell are you doing? You're renting it out without even asking me?"

"One – it's not your house, it's our house. Two – Morgan is my friend and needs a place to stay. I've offered her the carriage house."

8

"You should have asked me first. I don't want her here."

"I don't care." Lacey glared at him. "It'll do you some good to have another person around here. You spend too much time alone. Do you think Mom and Dad would want you to live alone in the dark? You hardly leave the farm anymore, Gabe. It's not healthy."

"I don't need you telling me what to do. I'm perfectly happy being out here by myself. I don't need a bunch of people looking at me and whispering behind my back. Nor do I need some woman living in my backyard and staring at me all day. Did you ever think I live out here alone because I'm tired of people staring at me? Tired of seeing the goddamn pity in their eyes?"

"Morgan isn't like that. She won't stare at you every time you walk by. Besides, you'll undoubtedly keep your distance from her just like you do everyone else."

"I don't keep my distance from you, Peter, or Nat," he protested.

"Don't you? When was the last time you came to the house, Gabe? Whenever we want to see you, we have to come here."

"Lacey, you don't get it. You don't have to -"

She put her hand up. "I'm not having this discussion with you. I get that you think you're a freak, and I get that you hate it when people stare at you, and, honey, I'm sorry. I really am. But I won't baby you anymore. I've tried it for too long, and it hasn't done anything but help you wallow in self-pity. You need to start living your life. I know it's hard, but I won't indulge you anymore. You need to rejoin the living, Gabriel."

Gabe stared in surprise at her. "Lacey, I can't -"

"You can and you will." She gave him a hard hug. "I love you and won't sit back and watch you wither away like this.

Enough is enough. Morgan is moving into the carriage house this weekend. She needs a place to stay, and she's a sweet girl. You won't even know she's here."

Gabe grunted, and Lacey squeezed his hand. "Also, we're having a barbeque this weekend, and you're coming. I mean it, Gabe."

CHAPTER 2

Morgan armed the sweat off her forehead and collapsed in the armchair. She was hot and sweaty, and her back hurt, but she was pleased with what she had accomplished. It was Saturday afternoon. She'd moved her meagre belongings into the carriage house this morning and spent the rest of the day cleaning the kitchen and removing the dust protectors from all of the furniture. Despite the breeze blowing through the open windows, it was hot and dirty work, and she sniffed her armpits. She would need to shower before going to the barbecue tonight.

She stood up and eyed the large couch. She decided it would look much better if she moved it to the other side of the room. She would move it and then have a quick shower.

She grabbed the arm of the couch and, with a loud grunt, pulled it across the room. It was even heavier than it looked, and she paused momentarily to catch her breath. There was a soft woof behind her.

The dog was back, and this time, it had brought a friend. The second dog was another Australian shepherd that was smaller in size and grey and white instead of brown. The larger dog woofed again at her.

"Hi, puppy. Who's your friend? And how did you get in here?"

It woofed again and approached her slowly. It sniffed her jean-covered thigh, and she petted the side of its neck. The second dog approached, already wagging its tail, and she also gave it a quick pat. "Since you're here, why don't you two help a girl out and push on the other end of the couch."

The dog chuffed, and she patted its head and grabbed the arm of the couch again. "Move back, puppy."

With another loud grunt, she pulled on the couch. It moved, but she was beginning to doubt her ability to move it across the room.

"Jeez Louise," she muttered. "What the heck are the cushions stuffed with? Rocks?"

"What are you doing?"

She shrieked in surprise at Gabe's deep voice. She staggered back, tripped over her own feet and fell. The back of her head hit the old wooden floor with a hard thud, and she cried out.

"Shit! Are you okay?" The right side of Gabe's face appeared above her, and she groaned and rubbed the back of her head.

"Just fine." She held out her hand. "Can you help me up?"

He hesitated and then took her hand. He yanked hard, and Morgan, not expecting it, tripped over her feet again as she staggered upward and slammed into his hard body. He yelped in surprise and stumbled back, still holding her hand. The arm of the couch hit the back of his knees, and he fell backward, dragging Morgan with him. They landed on the couch in a tangle of limbs, curses and dust. There was a deafening crack, and Morgan shrieked as the bottom of the sofa dropped from under them.

The dogs were barking loudly, and Gabe shouted, "Vincent! Delilah! Enough!"

They quieted immediately, and Morgan, coughing from the dust, took stock of the situation. The seat supports of the couch had snapped under their combined weight, and she and Gabe were wedged together at the bottom of the sofa. Her lower body was caught between the couch and Gabe's hard hip, and her upper half was sprawled across his upper chest. She tried to push away from him and felt a sliver of panic when she couldn't budge.

She cranked her neck when the dog snuffled her hair and licked her cheek.

"Vincent, leave," Gabe growled.

The dog woofed softly and retreated.

Morgan gave Gabe a worried look. "I've broken your couch. I'm so sorry. I'll replace it."

* * *

THE SOUND OF MORGAN'S VOICE DREW VINCENT OVER AGAIN. As Morgan turned to look at the dog, Gabe studied her closely. Dust covered her, and a large smear of dirt was across her forehead. Her light brown hair was pulled into a ponytail, and she giggled as Vincent licked her forehead.

"Good boy, Vincent. Get help. Tell them Timmy fell down the well." She laughed again, and the corners of Gabe's mouth twitched.

She was pretty, he decided. Her eyes were blue like his, but light instead of dark, and she had tanned skin and a nice curvy body. That curvy body was currently lying snugly on his, and his groin was embarrassingly aware of it. He dropped his gaze to where her breasts pressed against his chest. She was wearing a t-shirt with a scoop neckline, and he could see a hint of her cleavage. It was enough to make the blood rush to his dick, and he thanked God that her lower half was wedged beside him and not on top of him.

"Mr. Dern?" He realized he was still staring at her chest and quickly lifted his gaze. She was studying him, and he automatically turned his face so the left side was pressed against the cushion under his head.

A small frown line appeared in the smooth patch of flesh between her eyes. He was struck with the ridiculous urge to touch it with his fingers and try to smooth it away. He cleared his throat. Her eyes were still on his face, but they weren't looking at the ruined landscape of the left side, nor did he see any pity in them.

"Mr. Dern?" she said again, a tinge of worry in her voice. "Are you hurt?"

"No, and call me Gabe."

"I'm so sorry about your couch. I'm a real klutz, and I -"

"It's fine. It was an old couch."

"Are you sure?" She bit at her bottom lip, and he almost groaned out loud. He had a full-blown erection now, and he was ashamed of his lack of self-control. He had to get away from her before she looked down and saw the tell-tale bulge in his jeans. His dick had a mind of its own.

Can you blame it? You haven't had a woman touch you in years. Hell, you've never even –

He silenced his inner voice bitterly as she shifted, her breasts rubbing against his chest. "Um, I think we're really trapped in here."

"I just need to move to my side. Hold on," he grunted. He twisted under her, worming his way onto his side, and she gave a small squeak as her head banged against the side of the couch.

They were face-to-face now, both of them lying on their sides. Without thinking about it, he leaned forward, pressing against her and touching her head. "I'm sorry. Are you okay?"

14

"Yup. Stuff like this happens to me all the time. I'm a walking accident."

She laughed and moved her body experimentally. It made her pelvis rub against his, and Gabe could see the exact moment she realized he had an erection. Colour flooded her cheeks, and her pink lips pursed in surprise.

He groaned in embarrassment and pushed his way out of the couch. She hit her head again as he scrambled free, and he winced and took her arm, helping her out of the ruined remains of the sofa.

She dusted off her shirt, staring at the floor with pink cheeks. Gabe turned away and looked at the two dogs.

"I'm sorry," he rasped.

"It's fine." She cleared her throat.

His damn dick had finally decided to cooperate, and he turned back around, making sure to keep just the right side of his face in profile as he looked at her.

She was staring at the couch. "Gosh, I really am sorry about your couch. I shouldn't have tried to move it."

"It's not your fault. None of this would have happened if I hadn't scared you when I came in."

She cocked her head at him. "Why are you here anyway?"

"I came to see if the power was back on. I called yesterday to have it switched on."

"Oh. You know, I haven't even checked. Hit the light switch."

He flicked the switch by the door, and she smiled when the light came on. "Thanks for calling them."

"Yeah." He hesitated and then said, "The front door was wide open. We're a bit isolated in the country, but you should shut the door. There are coyotes and bears."

She frowned. "I'm sure I shut the door. Maybe it didn't latch properly."

"I'm sure you did shut it." Gabe eyed Vincent. "Were you being bad, Vincent?"

The dog ducked behind the couch, and Morgan gave Gabe a confused look. "I don't understand."

"Vincent knows how to open doors. If the door is unlocked, he can open the handle with his mouth."

"That's amazing!" Morgan clapped with delight as Vincent crowded up behind her. "You're the smartest puppy ever. Yes, you are, oh yes you are."

She crouched and petted the dog. Not to be ignored, Delilah nosed her way in. "Oh, you're a clever girl too, honey. Yes, you are."

Morgan kissed the top of Delilah's head as Vincent chuffed and head-butted her. She fell over with another loud thump, her elbow banging off the wooden floor. Gabe winced as Morgan popped to her feet, dusting her ass off with her hands.

"Whoops!" She rubbed vigorously at her elbow.

"Are you okay?"

"Yep." She glanced at her watch. "I should start getting ready for the barbeque, though. Did you want to drive in together?"

"I'm not going to the barbeque."

Morgan blinked at him. "Oh, I thought you were. Lacey said that you were going."

"She was wrong." He made a clicking noise with his tongue, and the two dogs followed him out of the living room.

* * *

When she heard the front door shut behind Gabe and the dogs, Morgan blew out her breath. The back of her head ached, and her elbow was stinging, but she barely noticed. The butterflies in her stomach – now those she noticed. She was no delicate flower. She knew exactly what that hardness was against her hip when Gabe pressed against her.

She started toward the bathroom, yanking her t-shirt over her head and tossing it through the open door of her bedroom. She knew she wasn't a raving beauty. She was of average height and weight, and her hair was a bland brown. She guessed that her eyes were her prettiest feature, but she was also blind as a bat. Without her contacts or glasses, she couldn't see five feet in front of herself. She really was just average.

She dated steadily through college, but afterward, there hadn't seemed to be enough time. She was starting a new career, her mother was sick, and dating fell to the side. Hell, she hadn't been laid in nearly three years.

That, she decided, was the reason she had felt an answering call of desire in her stomach when Gabe's erection pressed against her. Not that he wasn't handsome, she mused as she kicked off her jeans and left them in the hallway. His eyes were gorgeous and he had thick dark hair and what felt like an amazingly hard body. He'd be muscular – working on a farm was hard work. He would have muscles from lifting hay bales and stuff.

Did sheep eat hay?

She had no idea.

She closed her eyes and pictured Gabe's face. The right side was perfect – high cheekbone, full lips and a strong jaw. The left side – she winced a little. She hadn't seen much of it. Gabe did a remarkably good job of keeping it hidden, but she had seen enough.

She wasn't horrified by it like he probably thought she was. At her old school, a student's father had been burned in a house fire. His burns covered nearly all of his face, most of

17

his hair was gone, and his right ear was completely burned off.

His son was one of her "problem" students, and consequently, she had spent a great deal of time with both his mom and dad. At first, she found it difficult not to stare, but after a while, she didn't notice the scarring. The dad was friendly and funny and had a twisted sense of humour about his scars. Morgan had been a little envious of the obvious love between him and his wife.

She wondered how far Gabe's scarring went down. She'd only met him twice, but he was wearing a long-sleeve shirt buttoned to his neck both times. She shook her head. It didn't matter. Gabe was a borderline recluse with serious emotional issues. It was best to leave him be.

She glanced at her reflection in the bathroom mirror and sighed. Her face was streaked with dirt, she had dark circles under her eyes, and her hair was plastered to her skull with sweat. Why the hell Gabe had even gotten a stiffy after looking at her, she'd never know. Maybe he was attracted to the smell of sweat.

She quickly stripped off her bra and panties and started the shower. Despite being tired and dirty and smacking her head a record three times today, she was happy to be in such a perfect little house.

* * *

"Are you enjoying living in our small town, Morgan? It must be a big difference from the city." Andy smiled at her.

Morgan took a sip of beer. The barbecue was in full swing, and it hadn't taken long for the handsome blond man to start chatting her up. "I love it. Martinvale is a great little town. Have you lived here all your life?"

"I have," Andy said. "I thought about moving away in my

early twenties, but my girlfriend at the time convinced me not to."

He took his own sip of beer. "Ironically, two months after we broke up, she left Martinvale."

"I'm sorry."

He shrugged. "It was a long time ago. Speaking of girl-friends - would you like to have dinner with me this week?"

Morgan choked on her sip of beer. "Oh, I, um -"

Andy grinned at her. "Too forward?"

She laughed. "No. I was just surprised."

"I like to keep people on their toes. What do you say, Morgan? I promise I'll be charming and attentive and pay for dinner."

"Then I say yes."

"Great. Give me your number, and I'll text you on Monday." Andy grinned at her and took another drink of beer.

* * *

"Did you have fun tonight, Morgan?" Lacey smoothed plastic wrap over the leftover potato salad.

"I did. Thank you for inviting me." Morgan added another plate to the dishwasher.

"I saw you talking with Andy."

Morgan grinned. "He asked me out on a date."

"That's great." Lacey put the potato salad in the fridge and leaned against the counter. "Did you say yes?"

"I did." Morgan added more glasses to the top rack. "He seems like a nice guy."

"I don't know him well. He's a friend of one of Peter's co-workers, but he's super cute."

"He is, isn't he? I don't normally go for blonds, but he was charming."

"Good. How did unpacking today go?"

"Oh, fine. I broke the couch."

Lacey frowned. "You broke the couch?"

Morgan laughed. "Yep. Technically, your brother and I broke the couch, but I started it."

"Okay, explain yourself."

"I was trying to move the couch, and your brother's super smart dog broke into my house and brought his girlfriend with him. Then your brother stopped by and scared the crap out of me. I tripped, and he helped me up. I tripped again, and we both fell on the couch and crushed it. I'm trying not to take that as a sign that I need to lose weight."

Lacey laughed. "It was an old couch."

"That's what Gabe said, but I think he was just trying to be nice."

Lacey snorted. "Trust me, my brother is never nice just for the sake of being nice."

Morgan shrugged. "He seems nice enough to me. A bit rough around the edges, but I think that has more to do with him cutting himself off from everyone."

"Yeah," Lacey sighed. "Don't be mad, but part of my reason for offering the carriage house to you was so that my brother might have some human contact."

"I'm not mad." Morgan patted her arm. "Although I'm not sure it'll work. Your brother seems pretty intent on keeping everyone away."

"He wasn't always like that. He was such a sweet, friendly kid. He always wanted to be around others and help them however he could. He's great with animals. He was going to be a vet, and he would have been a damn good one."

"Can I ask what happened to him?" Morgan said.

Lacey took a deep breath. "When he was fifteen, he and some of his friends went for a drive. His best friend Tony had just gotten his driver's license, and so they, along with two other boys, took Tony's mom's car and went driving. A drunk driver hit them. The car caught on fire. Two of the boys died in the fire. Tony and Gabe were rescued, but both of them were terribly burned. Tony died two days later without ever waking up. Gabe nearly died, but he – he's so strong, you know? Always has been. He recovered, but he was left with horrible scarring."

"Is it all over his body?" Morgan asked.

Lacey shook her head. "No. It was just his upper body that was burned and mostly just the left side. It goes a little further onto the right side on his back, but they pulled him out of the car and put him out before it could go further down his body."

"Oh my goodness." Morgan couldn't imagine how much pain and suffering Gabe would have endured as he healed.

Lacey sat down at the table, her face pale and her hands trembling. "The doctor said he was quite lucky. His face was burned, but it missed his eye and ear. He could have been blinded or gone deaf. His chest and back got the worst of it, although, for a while there, they thought they might have to amputate his left arm."

Morgan sat down at the table and took Lacey's cold hands. "I'm sorry, Lacey."

"Yeah, me too. I wish you could have known him before this happened. His body healed, but emotionally, he just shut down. People talked and stared. It's such a small town, and he couldn't escape it. He gave up on the idea of being a vet and took online courses to become a website developer. He's successful at it but does all his work from home."

Lacey picked at one nail. "After Mom and Dad died, he became more and more withdrawn. Natalia drew him out of his shell for a bit, but she wasn't enough to bring him completely out of it. Now, he spends all of his time at the farm, only going into town when necessary, and I get more worried about him by the day. I've tried everything – sympathy, bullying, anger, tears – but nothing gets through to him. I had hoped he would come to the barbeque tonight, but I should have known better than to get my hopes up."

Morgan squeezed her hand as Lacey wiped away the tears dripping down her face. "Anyway, I'm hoping that with another human being out there, maybe he'll start to come out of his shell a bit."

Morgan smiled. "I'll do what I can."

"Thanks, Morgan. I appreciate that," Lacey said. " Now, enough of my crying - tell me where you're going with Andy on your date."

CHAPTER 3

She didn't notice him. He was sitting in the dark on the back porch, drinking a beer and staring at the garden when she walked past the house along the stone walkway. She hummed softly to herself, and he watched as she stopped to smell the lilac tree.

Vincent growled loudly, and before he could stop him, the dog bounded off the porch toward her. He barked once, and she jumped before turning toward the dog.

"Vincent, hush! It's just me." The dog's growling turned to a low, pleased whine, and she giggled when he head-butted her leg.

"What are you doing up so late, puppy?" She rubbed his head and started walking again. Vincent was weaving around her feet and as she disappeared into the darkness toward the carriage house, Gabe took another drink of beer.

Tomorrow would be a week since she moved in. He stayed away from her, but she sought him out a few times while he worked in the garden, chatting politely to him as he weeded. He kept his replies short and used his body language to tell her he wasn't interested in talking. She ignored his silent hints, and he finally started working in the garden during the day when she was at work.

There was a muffled thump, and Morgan groaned. Vincent started barking, and she hurriedly hushed him. Gabe hesitated and then stood and started down the steps. Delilah trailed after him as Morgan groaned again.

"Ouch! Son of a biscuit!"

He hurried down the path and stared in disbelief. Morgan was tangled in the large rose bushes planted along the stone pathway.

"What the hell?" he said, ignoring her gasp of surprise. "How the hell did you end up in the rose bushes?"

"Your dog tripped me." She glared at him as she struggled out of the bushes. She hissed in pain as thorns scraped across her bare arm.

"Oh, for God's sake." He reached down, ignoring the thorns that caught on the sleeves of his shirt, and helped her out of the bushes.

"Can you walk twenty feet without falling?" he muttered.

"It was dark, okay? Besides, I told you I was clumsy." She picked a thorn out of her arm and winced.

He sighed. Even in the dark, he could see the blood streaming down her arms. He took her wrist and led her toward the farmhouse. "Come on."

She didn't argue and allowed him to lead her back down the path and up the back porch steps. He opened the screen door, and she followed him into the kitchen.

"Sit down." He pointed to one of the kitchen chairs, and she sat down. He opened a cupboard and pulled out a first-aid kit.

* * *

MORGAN STARED AT HER ARMS. BLOOD TRICKLED IN THIN streams, and scratches from the thorns covered them. Her face stung, and she touched her cheek gingerly, not surprised when her fingers came away bloody.

Gabe pulled up a chair and sat across from her, their knees nearly touching. He examined her left arm, pulling out a few small thorns and dropping them on the table as Vincent, joined by Delilah, put his head on Morgan's lap. Gabe ran his fingers over her right arm, and she shivered a little at his warm touch. Mistaking it for a shiver of pain, he apologized.

"It's fine." She cleared her throat. "Thank you for rescuing me from the roses. I'm sorry I crushed them."

He shrugged. "I was thinking of taking them out anyway." He opened a bottle of peroxide and ripped open a package of gauze.

"Really? But roses are so pretty. Why would you rip them out?"

"I'd think you'd want them gone. Odds are you'll fall into them again sooner or later."

She laughed. "Good point. Maybe I should start wrapping myself in bubble wrap?"

He grunted, and she grinned again. "The fourth time I fell off the jungle gym, my mom threatened to send me to school in a helmet and protective padding. I could only convince her not to by promising never to set foot on the jungle gym again."

He poured a bit of peroxide onto the gauze. "Maybe you should turn on the porch light so you can see when you're walking down the path."

"The light's burned out," she said. "I would have changed it, but I'm too short to reach it, and I tend to avoid stepping onto chairs or stools."

"Probably a wise idea," he said. "This will hurt."

He dabbed the scratches on her arms with the peroxide-soaked gauze. She hissed again with pain.

"Sorry."

"That's okay." She studied his face in the light. Engrossed in cleaning her arm, it was the first time he wasn't actively hiding the left side of his face from her. She stared at the scars that marred his face. Half of his left eyebrow was missing, as was the hair at his temple. No hair grew on the marred skin, and she supposed that was why he kept the right side of his face and upper lip so closely shaved. The burns had come incredibly close to his left eye, and his bottom lip pulled slightly to the left because of the scarred skin.

She quickly looked down at her arms when he raised his head, knowing he would be embarrassed if he saw her looking at him. He took a new piece of gauze, soaked it in peroxide, and worked on her left arm.

"I'll change the light for you tomorrow," he suddenly said.

"Thank you. I really appreciate that. I'll probably still trip, but at least I'll be able to see when I'm picking myself up out of the rose bushes." She grinned at him, and his lips twitched in response.

"Why, Mr. Dern, is that a smile?"

This time, he really smiled, revealing even white teeth, and she gave him a delighted look. "You have great teeth."

He blushed, and she patted his arm. "Aww, you're blushing. Seriously, though – great teeth. Did you have braces?"

"Yeah, two years."

"Me too. Wasn't the tightening part awful? Gosh, I used to moan and complain something awful when I had to go in and have them tightened."

He just shrugged and swiped at one of the scratches. Without looking at her, he said, "Were you out with Andy tonight?"

She twitched a little. "I was. How did you know about Andy?"

"Small town. News travels fast."

She laughed. "I guess I'm used to the city where no one knows your name and couldn't care less about your business."

"I didn't mean to be nosy."

"You weren't," she said hastily. "I'm not trying to hide it or anything. I met Andy at your sister's barbecue last weekend. He asked me to dinner, and we had a good time, so I accepted his invitation to see a movie tonight."

"What movie did you see?"

"A really awful horror one. Just between us - I think Andy was expecting that I would squeal and latch onto him in terror. I should have told him that I don't scare easily, and then maybe we could have gone to the comedy I suggested."

He finished wiping her arms and sat back. "There you go."

"Thanks again, Gabe. I appreciate your help." She smiled at him, and he hesitated.

"Wait. Your face is bleeding, too."

He took the final piece of gauze and soaked it in peroxide. Morgan leaned forward and closed her eyes. He wiped gently at the scratch on her cheek. She flinched a little when the peroxide bubbled.

"I'm sorry," he said.

She opened her eyes. Their faces were so close she knew Gabe could see the rims of her contact lenses. He continued to wipe at her cheek without tearing his gaze from hers. His pupils became darker and larger until only a tiny bit of blue showed.

She parted her lips and wondered if he could feel her trembling. When he dipped his head, moving his mouth toward hers, she made a low sound of encouragement. Just before his mouth touched hers, he jerked his head back.

He dropped the gauze on the table and shoved his chair back before standing and turning away from her. "I'm finished."

Morgan released her breath slowly and stood up. "Thank you." When he didn't turn around, she walked to the door. "Good night, Gabe."

"Good night, Morgan."

* * *

"HI, MS. WILSON!"

"Hello, Natalia." Morgan smiled at the little girl who bounded into the barn.

"What are you doing?"

"I'm trying to pet the kittens, but they're too afraid."

Natalia sat beside her and peered at the huddle of kittens in the corner of the empty stall. "They're afraid of everyone but Uncle Gabe. Mama says he has a gift with animals."

"Is your mom here?"

"Yep. She went to the house to find Uncle Gabe. Guess what?"

"What?"

"I finished my project on the lions."

"That's great! It's not due until Wednesday."

"I know, but Mama said if I did it this weekend, I would have Monday night and Tuesday night to do whatever I wanted."

"She's a very wise woman." Morgan smoothed the little girl's soft hair and then made another clicking noise with her tongue. "Here, kitty, kitty."

"Do you like living here, Ms. Wilson?"

"I do. It's very peaceful, and the carriage house is a nice place to live."

"Mama and Daddy used to live in it before I was born," Natalia said.

"I know, your mom told me."

The little girl picked up a piece of straw and broke it in two. "Do you like my Uncle Gabe?"

"I do, honey. He's nice." She stared at the scratches on her arms, remembering last night when she had come this close to planting one on him.

"Will you ask him to come to the school play?"

"Honey, I think you should ask him." Morgan smiled at the little girl.

"I already did. He said he would think about it, but that means no. It always means no whenever Daddy says he'll think about it."

The little girl sighed and dug a hole in the straw. "Uncle Gabe never comes to anything."

Morgan hesitated, unsure what to say, but the little girl didn't wait for a reply. "Mama says it's because people stare at his scars. I don't know why they do that. I don't see anything weird about them."

"Sometimes people stare because they're uncomfortable and don't know what to say because he looks a bit different," Morgan said.

"Yeah, I guess. But I wish he would come to see me in the play." Natalia inched toward the kittens. They hissed and arched their backs, and she stopped. "We need Uncle Gabe."

"Need Uncle Gabe for what?" Gabe stuck his head into the stall.

"Hi, Uncle Gabe!" Natalia grinned at him. "We want to pet the kittens. Come sit with us so they'll come over."

Morgan moved over so there was room for him to sit between them. She gave him a tentative smile. "Good morning, Gabriel."

"Hello, Morgan." He sat so that his right side was facing

her and made the same clicking noise with his tongue that she had done. Instead of retreating further into the stall, the six kittens stretched and crept closer.

"Be very quiet and don't move, Nat," Gabe said.

The little girl leaned against his leg and did as he asked. Morgan watched with amazement as, one by one, the kittens climbed into Gabe's lap. All of them purred loudly as he stroked and rubbed their soft fur. A tiny orange one sat on his knee and batted at Natalia's silky hair. She giggled and carefully petted the kitten. It arched its back and butted its face against hers.

"Here." Gabe handed Morgan a tiny black kitten, and she cupped it in her hands. Its eyes were still blue, and it stared curiously at her. She rubbed its small head and grinned delightedly when it purred.

"They're so sweet. I always wanted a cat, but my mom was allergic."

"Where does your mama live, Ms. Wilson?"

"She died, honey."

"Oh. Do you miss her?" Natalia asked.

Morgan nodded. "I do. But she was very sick before she died, and I feel better knowing that she isn't sick anymore."

"I bet she's in heaven with Grandma and Grandpa." The little girl used a piece of straw to tickle the kitten sitting in her lap.

"I bet she is too."

"Did the girl sheep have their babies yet?" Natalia asked Gabe.

"Not yet. But I'll be moving them into the jugs soon."

"Jugs?" Morgan asked.

"Separate pens in the sheep shed. I move the ewes into them when they're about to give birth so they can have some time alone with their lambs."

"Do they have more than one lamb at a time?"

"Usually, yeah. Twins are pretty common, and occasionally triplets are born."

"How many are having babies this year, Uncle Gabe?" Natalia was trailing a piece of straw for the kittens to chase.

"Just two, Nat."

"Why only two?" Morgan asked.

Gabe shrugged. "The sheep farming is just a hobby. I don't want to have too many. I don't sell them for meat purposes, so if I don't sell them to other hobby farms or 4H groups, the sheep are with me for their life. I only have so much room."

"Do you make any money from them?"

He nodded. "Yes. I shear them every year and sell their wool."

Morgan looked around the empty barn. The sheep were kept in a separate, larger barn when they weren't grazing in the fenced-in pasture, and she wondered what this smaller barn was for.

As if he had read her mind, Gabe said, "I used to have a couple of cows and a few horses."

"Nat, honey, are you ready to go?" Lacey popped into the stall and smiled at Morgan. "Hello, Morgan."

"Hey, Lacey. How are you?"

"Good."

"Look at the kittens, mama. They're getting big."

"They sure are." Lacey stroked her daughter's hair. "Time to go, sweetie."

"Uncle Gabe, will you come to the park with us? Mama said we could play in the park, and then we're going to a movie this afternoon," Natalia pleaded.

"I can't, Nat. I'm going to the auction today."

"Oh. Ms. Wilson, do you want to come with us?" Natalia smiled at her.

"Actually, if it's okay with your Uncle Gabe, I'll tag along to the auction."

Gabe stared at her in surprise, and she flushed a little. "I've never been to an auction before."

"It's not that interesting," he said.

Her blush deepened, but she persisted. "I still wouldn't mind going. Unless you don't want me to come?"

He hesitated. Morgan was almost certain he would refuse to let her go with him, and she had to hide her surprise when he said, "That's fine. I'm leaving in about half an hour."

* * *

"ARE YOU BUYING ANYTHING TODAY?" MORGAN STOOD NEXT to Gabe at the auction and craned her neck to stare at him. She wasn't short, but Gabe was well over six feet.

He shook his head. "Nah, probably not. I like to go to keep an eye on what's out there."

She nodded. She was standing on his right side, a move he carefully orchestrated. She pretended not to notice. She'd seen a few people staring curiously at Gabe's face, but she had pretended not to notice that either. She had a feeling that he was uncomfortable being out with her in public, and she didn't want to do anything that would make it worse.

"Do you sell your sheep here?"

He shook his head again. "No. If I sold them here, they would go for meat. I don't want that."

"Why not?"

"I've raised most of my flock since they were babies. I don't want them slaughtered for food."

She smiled. "For someone who always acts so gruff, you're a real softie. It's sweet."

He blushed, and she poked him lightly on the side. "Also, it's kind of adorable how much you blush."

"I don't blush."

"Of course you don't."

The auctioneer called for the next animal, and the crowd around them pushed closer to the viewing section. A large man wearing a plaid shirt and cowboy hat brushed past her, bonking her in the head with his elbow and pushing her into Gabe.

"You okay?" Gabe scowled at the man as she leaned against his arm and rubbed her head.

"I'm fine." She strained to see over the people in front of her.

* * *

GABE WAS STARTING TO REGRET ALLOWING MORGAN TO COME with him. He'd been to the auction enough times that most people didn't stare anymore, but there were always a few new people. He didn't want her to see them staring at his ruined face. But the way she'd smiled so hopefully at him made him unable to resist her request. With a small trickle of dismay, he realized that he couldn't say no to her.

She leaned closer as she strained to see over the people standing in front of them. He wished she would move away. Her arm was touching his arm, causing not entirely unpleasant sensations in his belly. It had been years since he had allowed anyone but Lacey and Nat close to him, and her casual disregard for his personal space was both exciting and disturbing. He shifted a little, but instead of moving away, she shifted with him. She smelled good, a light floral scent that clung to her.

She gasped, and he followed her gaze to the animal in the viewing pen. It was a small brown cow with white blotches, and he frowned when Morgan pushed her way to the front. He followed her and stood behind her as she gazed at it.

"The poor thing," she murmured.

The man led the cow into the middle of the pen. She was limping, and her ribs were visible. Her udder was cracked with streaks of dried blood, and her right eye was missing. She mooed pitifully as the auctioneer began.

The crowd stepped back, they had lost interest almost immediately, and she glanced up at him. "Poor little cow. What will happen to her if no one buys her?"

He paused. "She's in bad shape. Most likely, she'll end up in the slaughterhouse."

She gave a low sigh of distress and turned back to stare at the cow. "Poor baby. She doesn't look very old."

As the auctioneer gamely called out numbers, trying to entice someone to purchase the beast, Gabe studied Morgan. She was leaning against the pen, staring sadly at the cow. He had never seen her anything but happy and cheerful, and his stomach twisted.

Quickly, before he could change his mind, he raised his hand. The auctioneer nodded and immediately called 'sold' in a loud voice.

Her back to him, Morgan had missed the entire exchange. She turned around and squeezed his arm. "Someone bought her!"

He nodded, and she smiled at him. "I hope she goes to a good home." She watched as the cow was led out of the pen.

The crowd was dispersing, and she frowned. "Is the auction over?"

"Yeah. Listen, I -"

Her phone rang, and she pulled it out, smiling a little at the number. "Excuse me for a moment, please, Gabe."

She hit the answer button on her phone. "Hi, Andy. I'm good. How are you?"

She listened and then smiled. "I'm at the auction with

Gabe. Yep, the auction. Tonight? Sure, I'd love to. I can meet you at the restaurant around six if you'd like?"

Gabe touched her arm. "I'll meet you at the truck in ten minutes, okay?"

She nodded and gave him a thumbs-up before continuing her conversation.

Gabe walked away, trying to ignore the niggle of jealousy in his stomach. It was stupid to be jealous of Andy. Morgan was dating Andy, and she wasn't interested in being anything but a friend to Gabe. And even that, he wasn't so sure about. He had a bad feeling his sister had sent her to live in the carriage house because she was worried and felt sorry for him. He sighed harshly. He didn't need anyone's pity.

He tamped down the thread of anger. He had to pay for the damn cow and make arrangements to pick it up tomorrow with the trailer. He was already regretting buying the thing. It looked close to death and would probably cost him an arm and a leg in vet bills.

CHAPTER 4

The next morning, Gabe found her on the front porch of the carriage house. She was drinking a cup of coffee and looked tired and out of sorts.

"Morning, Morgan."

"Hey, Gabe." She gave him a distracted smile as he climbed the stairs and sat gingerly in the wicker chair beside hers.

"How was your date with Andy last night?" He wasn't used to making small talk, and it felt awkward and strange.

"Fine. I guess."

He frowned. "Did something happen?"

She didn't answer, and he frowned again. "Morgan?"

"Hmm? No, it was good – mostly." She took another sip of coffee and stared moodily into the garden.

He cleared his throat. He wondered if he was supposed to ask her again if something had happened. He decided he'd better not, even though he was intensely curious. "Do you have a minute? I have something I want to show you in the barn."

He'd risen early this morning and taken the trailer to pick up the cow.

"What is it?" she asked.

"It's uh, it's kind of a surprise."

"I like surprises." She gave him a more natural smile and set her coffee cup on the small table beside her chair before following him to the barn.

She stopped at the door and grinned up at him. "Should I close my eyes?"

"Um, yeah, okay."

She closed her eyes and held out her hand. He stared at it for a moment before realizing what she wanted. His hands were suddenly sweaty, and he wiped them on his jeans before taking her small hand in his large one. She gripped it firmly, and a tingle went through his entire body.

He opened the door to the barn and led her inside to the stall where he'd put the cow. It was staring silently at him, and he sighed inwardly. He would get the vet to stop by tomorrow, and there was a good chance he would tell him the cow should be put out of its misery. He should have waited until hearing what the vet had to say before showing Morgan the cow, but it was too late now. She was standing next to him, a small smile on her mouth and her hand still holding his hand.

"Open your eyes," he said.

She opened them and gasped in surprise. "The cow!"

She stared up at him, her face filled with sweet delight, and he was suddenly very glad he had bought the poor beast.

"You bought her?" She squeezed his hand, and he nodded. "Yeah."

"I had no idea!" She surprised him by giving him a brief, hard hug. "Thank you so much for buying her!"

He nodded and turned away from her, willing his erection to go away. Morgan had only hugged him for a few seconds, but it was enough to make his dick stand up and take notice. Christ, he was a pervert.

Morgan moved away and studied the cow. "Poor girl." She paused and eyed the blood-streaked udder. "It is a girl, right?"

He laughed. "Yeah, it's a girl."

She blushed. "Sorry, I'm such a city girl."

"It's fine." He stood next to her as she leaned against the stall door.

"Do you think she's friendly?"

He shrugged. "She seemed friendly enough when I loaded her into the trailer this morning."

He scooped out a handful of grain from a nearby container. "Here, try giving her some of this."

She held out her hand, and he poured the grain into the palm of it. "Hold your hand straight and keep your fingers out of the way."

She nodded a bit nervously as he opened the door of the stall. She slipped in and whispered, "Good cow. Good girl. Here, try some grain."

She held her hand out, and the cow sniffed delicately at the grain before eating it from her hand. She gave Gabe an excited look. "She likes it!"

He smiled a little. "Not surprising. She probably hasn't had a good meal in ages."

The cow finished eating the grain, and Morgan stroked the side of her neck a bit timidly. "What do you think happened to her?"

"I don't know. She's had a rough life, though, I think."

"Yeah." Growing bolder, she patted and stroked the cow on the side of her body. "She's so bony."

"We'll fatten her up in no time." He entered the stall and petted the cow on her forehead. She sniffed his shirt pocket, found nothing interesting, and turned her head to stare at Morgan.

"I wonder how she lost her eye." Morgan rubbed the cow's broad nose. The cow leaned against her and pushed her into the side of the stall.

"Ouch!" She winced, but when Gabe went to push the cow out of the way, she shook her head. "No, don't. She's just enjoying the attention, I think."

Humming softly, she petted and stroked the cow. "What's her name?"

"You can name her whatever you want."

"Daisy," she said immediately. "Daisy is a good cow name."

She stared at the cow's swollen leg and her missing eye before looking solemnly at him. "Do you think she'll make it?"

"I'll have the vet look at her tomorrow. She's eating and showing interest in her surroundings. That's a good sign."

She rested her head on the cow's side for a moment. "I hope so."

She gave the cow a final pat before Gabe pushed the cow back so she could slip out of the stall. He shut the stall door, and they left the barn. As they crossed the yard, she smiled at him. "Natalia's school play is Wednesday night."

He grunted in reply, and she said, "She really wants you to go."

"Yeah. I can't make it."

"What if there was an alternative to sitting in the audience? Would you go then?"

"What do you mean?"

"If you didn't have to sit with everyone else, would you go?"

"Maybe," he said cautiously.

She grinned. "Good. I'll be at the side door to the school

ten minutes before the play starts. If you want to see her in the play, meet me there, okay?"

"Can I think about it?"

"Sure, but I hope you'll come. It would mean a lot to Natalia."

* * *

THE LOOK OF DELIGHT ON MORGAN'S FACE WHEN SHE OPENED the side door and saw him standing in the shadows made Gabe very glad he showed up. "Gabriel, hi! You came!"

"Yeah."

She held her hand out. "Follow me."

He paused and then took her hand and let her lead him into the building.

They walked silently down the empty hallway. Gabe felt like he should let go of Morgan's hand, but she gripped it firmly, and he didn't know if it would be rude to shake free of her touch. Just touching her hand excited him, making his stomach churn with nervousness and something else he didn't recognize.

He felt relieved and disappointed when she released his hand and used a key to open a plain grey door. "Follow me, Mr. Dern."

She gave him a small grin of excitement, and he followed her into the dark. He could hear children laughing and talking in low murmurs of excitement, and she took his hand again, leading him around a few boxes before stopping next to a curtain.

"Where are we?"

"Backstage. I thought you could watch the play from back here. There won't be anyone else around to," she paused, "bug you."

He gave her a look of gratefulness. "I – thank you, Morgan."

"You're welcome. It helps to have friends connected with the theatre scene." She winked and dropped his hand. "Hold on a minute. I'll be right back."

She left him standing by the curtain and melted into the darkness. It wasn't long before she returned. He could hear Natalia's voice, and he smiled a little.

"Ms. Wilson, the play is starting soon."

"I know, honey. I have a surprise for you. It'll only take a minute."

The grin spread on his face as Morgan appeared before him, leading Natalia by the hand.

Natalia cried out with surprise and hugged him fiercely, her thin arms squeezing his waist. "Uncle Gabe! You're here!"

"Hi, Nat." He returned her hug and kissed the top of her head. She was dressed like a fairy, complete with transparent wings on her back and a garland of flowers around her head. "You look pretty."

"Thanks, Uncle Gabe! I'm a fairy princess!" She held her dress out and twirled in a circle.

"You're the prettiest fairy princess I've ever seen." He kissed her head again as she giggled.

"Are you going to sit with Mama and Daddy?"

"Um…"

"Honey, I've asked your Uncle Gabe to watch the play backstage with me so I wouldn't be lonely," Morgan said.

"That's so nice of him," Natalia said.

"It is," Morgan agreed. She patted Natalia on her arm. "Okay, sweetheart, you had better return to the rest of your class. Good luck!"

"Thanks, Ms. Wilson. Bye, Uncle Gabe!" She blew them both a kiss and ran off as Morgan smiled at Gabe.

"I should have brought popcorn."

He grinned at her. At some point, smiling at her had become as natural as smiling at Natalia. "I've got some mints in my pocket."

She laughed. "Don't be stingy – pass them over."

He dug in his pocket and gave her the mints. She popped one in her mouth and handed the mints back. The curtains drew back, and she smiled. "Enjoy the show."

* * *

"CHEESE AND CRACKERS!" MORGAN BENT AND PICKED UP THE fallen laundry. It had been pouring rain for most of the day, and she had just spilled her freshly washed laundry all over the muddy driveway.

She sighed as she threw her clothes into the laundry basket. The carriage house was great, and she loved it, but it didn't have a washer and dryer, so she had to lug her laundry to the Laundromat to wash her clothes. Tripping had just cost her two hours, and now she had to head directly back into town to clean them again.

"What are you doing?"

Gabe and the dogs had come out of the barn, and she shooed Delilah and Vincent away from her clothes.

"I tripped and spilled my laundry. Now I'm heading back into town to wash them again," she said grumpily.

"You can use the washer and dryer in my house if you'd like," Gabe offered.

"Really? Are you sure you wouldn't mind?"

"Nope." He took the basket of laundry from her and started toward the house. She followed along behind him as the dogs bounded ahead.

"Thank you so much, Gabe. You have no idea how much I appreciate this."

"Yeah, no problem."

They entered the house, and he pointed to the dog beds in the living room and made the hand motion for the dogs to lie down. They went immediately to their beds, and she slipped off her shoes before following him to the laundry room.

"Ooh, this is nice."

He grunted. "It's just a washer and dryer."

"Yeah, but when you spend two hours in a Laundromat, and some guy sits next to you and picks his nose the entire time, this is a little slice of heaven." She laughed.

She squeezed by him, ignoring the way he twitched. The laundry room was small, and she wondered if he was staring at her ass in her tight jeans.

She dumped the entire basket of clothes into the washing machine and grinned when Gabe said, "Aren't you going to separate them into darks, colours and whites?"

"Nah. I like to live life on the edge. Besides, what's the worst that can happen? My white underwear turns pink? I like pink."

He flushed at the mention of her panties, and she grinned. "I've embarrassed you."

"No, you haven't," he replied curtly. "Excuse me. I was just about to start dinner."

* * *

HIS FACE RED, GABE BEAT A HASTY RETREAT TO THE KITCHEN. He started the pot of stock on the stove before cutting up the vegetables for the soup. It wasn't long before she joined him in the kitchen. She leaned against the counter and watched him chop the vegetables methodically and add them to the pot on the stove.

"Whatcha' cookin'?" she asked.

"Soup."

"It smells good." She leaned over the pot and inhaled deeply. "Really good."

He rinsed the knife off and didn't reply.

"I'm starving." She smiled at him.

"Would you, uh, like to stay for supper?"

He groaned inwardly. Why did he say that?

"I thought you'd never ask." She grinned at him and washed her hands. "What can I do to help?"

"You can grab the spices from the cupboard over there." He pointed to one of the top cupboards before turning on the tap and rinsing the potatoes.

"Okey, dokey." Morgan opened the cupboard. The spices were on the top shelf, and she stretched to reach them, her t-shirt riding up.

"What happened to your back?" He hadn't meant to ask her that, just like he hadn't meant to cross the kitchen and stand beside her.

"Huh?" She looked down. "Well, would you look at that – that's a good one."

"What did you do?" He stared at the large, black and purple bruise on the pale skin of her back.

"I don't know."

"How could you not know?" He went to touch the bruise before stopping and clasping his hands tightly behind his back.

She shrugged. "I fall a lot, remember?"

"Morgan, this one looks really bad. Did you go to the doctor?"

"Gosh, no. If I went to the doctor every time I hurt myself, I'd be there 24/7."

She suddenly brightened. "Oh, now I remember. I slipped in the tub a couple of days ago. Fell right back against the faucet and whacked my head a good one on the wall. I really have to get some of those anti-slip things for the bottom of the tub."

He returned to the potatoes. "I've never met anyone who falls as much as you do."

"I know, right? I'm like a darn cartoon character. I used to be embarrassed, but now I just go with it."

"Have you ever broken anything?"

"Oh yes. I've broken my arms - my right one twice - and my ankle. Oh, and I cracked my ribs once. I fell out of my cousin's tree house."

"I can't believe your parents let you go in a tree house."

"It's always been just my mom and me. My dad died when I was a baby. She forbade me to go into the tree house. I decided to do it anyway." She wiggled her eyebrows at him. "My middle name is Danger."

He laughed as he added the potatoes to the pot.

"It wasn't as bad as the time my cousin and I were running through the park, though. I tripped and fell right into a tree. One of its branches snapped off under my weight and skewered me in the side. Look at this."

He glanced over as she raised her t-shirt and showed him the scar on her right side. "Impressive, right?"

He nodded, swallowing thickly. He wanted to drop to his knees and kiss the pale, round scar, run his tongue over the slightly raised flesh while he gripped her firm thighs and inhaled her scent. He realized she was still talking and forced himself to concentrate.

"I walked home with this branch sticking out of my side, blood oozing out around it, and my cousin stopping every five minutes to barf from the sight of my blood. My mother nearly had a stroke when we walked through the door."

She brought him the spices and he added them to the soup as she stood next to him and watched. He stirred it carefully, and she inhaled again. "Oh man, that smells so good. I skipped lunch."

"How come you're not out with Andy tonight?"

Christ, he hadn't meant to ask that.

She shrugged. "I hung out with him last night and Thursday night. He wanted to come over, but I said no. I like my space, you know?"

He nodded as she boosted herself up and sat on the counter, swinging her legs idly. "We're going to his parents' house tomorrow night for Sunday night dinner."

He grunted in surprise, and she raised her eyebrows. "Too soon, yeah? We've been going out for three weeks, and I'm meeting his parents already? I once dated a guy for nearly eight months before he introduced me to his parents. Is moving this quickly a small town guy thing or what?"

"I wouldn't know," he said.

She sighed. "I tried to get out of it, but Andy was insistent. I guess we'll see if I embarrass myself. Of course, it's not like I haven't tripped and fallen flat on my face in front of people before."

The little frown line appeared between her eyes. "Hmm, I think I'd better wear pants. Flashing your underwear does not make a good impression on the parents."

"Yeah, probably not."

"How's Daisy doing tonight?" she asked.

"She's good. The swelling in her leg is almost gone, and the infection in her eye socket has cleared up nicely."

The vet had given Daisy a surprisingly good chance, and after only a week, she had improved so much that he was letting her into the pasture to graze with the sheep. Every night, Morgan visited with her, feeding her grain and hay and brushing her. She was a sweet and gentle cow, and he had to admit it was nice to have one in the barn again.

"That's great. I'll go to the barn in the morning and give

her a good brushing. I think she recognizes me now." She gave him a grin of delight.

"I'm sure she does. Cows are much smarter than people think."

"Do you think she'll start producing milk?" she asked.

"If we breed her and she has a calf, she will."

"Will you breed her?"

He shrugged. "Maybe. She's still pretty young, so it's possible if she's healthy enough."

"A baby cow would be so sweet. If she does have a baby, will you teach me to milk her?"

"If you'd like."

"I really would," she said enthusiastically. "My mom would laugh so hard if she could see me living in the country and learning to milk a cow."

"How did your mom die?" he asked and then winced. "Sorry, that's not my business."

"I don't mind you asking," she said. "She had liver cancer."

"I'm sorry."

"Me too. I miss her a lot." There were a few moments of silence, and then she smiled at him. "How old are you?"

"Twenty-nine. How old are you?"

"Twenty-seven. You've lived here your entire life?"

He nodded. "Yeah. Why did you leave the city?"

She shrugged. "After my mom died, it just didn't feel like home anymore. The house was too empty, and the city felt too big, you know? I found the job ad here in Martinvale. It was a bit unusual because I started halfway through the year. I guess the previous teacher had to move for her husband's job. Anyway, I applied, got the job, and here I am."

"Here you are," he echoed.

"Did the sheep have their babies yet?" she asked as he stirred the soup.

"The one did. I think the other one will probably give birth this week."

"Really? When did she give birth?"

He smiled at the excitement in her voice. "Friday night. She had twins."

"Oh my gosh! Could I see them?"

"Sure. I'll take you out to the barn after supper."

She jumped down from the counter and squeezed his upper arm. "Thanks, Gabe!"

He nodded, his skin tingling from her touch even through his long-sleeve shirt, and stirred the soup again.

"I'm going to go see if my laundry is done." She left the kitchen, and he exhaled in a harsh rush. He didn't want to admit to himself how much he enjoyed her company, but it was getting harder to deny.

He sighed and tasted the soup. There was no harm in being friends with her, and if he had a little crush – so what? It was to be expected. She was pretty and friendly, and she was the first woman who didn't stare at him with a combination of pity and disgust. In fact, he had the oddest feeling that she didn't even really notice the scars on his face. Hell, he had even sort of forgotten about trying to actively hide the left side of his face from her tonight.

He snorted. She might be used to the scars on his face, but they were mild compared to the ones on his arm and upper body. He would be wise to remember just how grotesque he looked before he started imagining touching Morgan and having her touch him in return.

Besides, she was dating Andy.

CHAPTER 5

G abe stood and stretched before calling the dogs. It was Sunday night, and he wanted to check on Molly one last time before bed. He didn't expect her to give birth tonight, but it wouldn't hurt to check on her once more.

He left the house, the dogs trotting in front of him. He looked to the carriage house, like he always did now, and frowned when he saw a small glowing ember in the darkness. What was that? He paused and then headed toward it. He knew Morgan was home, he had heard her car pulling into the driveway close to an hour ago, but the carriage house was dark.

The dogs ran ahead of him, and his heart sped up in his chest when he heard Morgan's soft voice.

"Hello, puppies."

He climbed the steps; his eyes had adjusted to the dark, and he could see Morgan sitting in one of the wicker chairs. His mouth dropped open when he realized the glowing ember he had seen was from the cigarette she was smoking.

He dropped into the chair beside hers. "Hey, Morgan."

"Hello, Gabe," she replied listlessly. She took a deep drag of the cigarette and blew smoke rings out.

"Is there something wrong?"

"Why do you ask?"

"You seem upset."

She shrugged. "Yeah, maybe."

He drummed his fingers nervously on the arm of his chair. "I didn't know you smoked."

"I've smoked off and on since I was eighteen." She inhaled deeply on the cigarette and blew the smoke out before staring moodily into the darkness. "It's a disgusting habit, I know."

He stayed silent, and after a moment, she glanced at him. "Surprised?"

"Yeah. You seem so – so…"

"Goody-two shoes? Little miss sweetie pie?" She arched her eyebrow at him.

He nodded. "Pretty much. I've never even heard you curse."

"When you work with kids, it's best to keep the swearing to a minimum." She stubbed out the cigarette and reached for the pack sitting on the table. She struck a match and lit another. Before she blew out the match, he had enough time to see her crying.

"Please tell me what's wrong, Morgan," he said.

She took another drag on the cigarette and blew it out in a harsh rush. "Andy dumped me tonight."

He blinked in surprise. "What? Why?"

"He said it was because I didn't seem interested enough in him. He said I would want to spend more time with him if I liked him as much as he liked me."

She took another angry drag. "Apparently, old Andy felt we should be surgically attached at the hip."

She stared at him. "I'm not supposed to enjoy my alone

time in a new relationship? That makes me some kind of freak?"

He shook his head. "No, I don't think so."

"Yeah." She pulled her feet up and wrapped her arms around her knees. "He's a big fat liar swimming in horse poop."

He laughed, he couldn't help it, and she gave him a mock scowl. "He is."

"What do you mean?"

"His reasons for breaking up with me are big fat lies." She puffed on her cigarette. "You want to know the real reason the butthead broke up with me?"

"Sure."

"I wouldn't have sex with him."

He jerked a little, but she didn't notice. "You want to know the ironic part? I probably would have slept with him if he hadn't made it so apparent that he expected me to sleep with him. According to him, city girls are tramps who can't resist jumping a sweet old country boy's bones."

She scoffed and took one final drag before stubbing out her cigarette. "Do you expect a girl to sleep with you in the first three weeks?"

"I – uh…"

She sighed. "Never mind. It's not fair to compare you to him – you're a sweetheart, and he's a butthead."

He didn't know what to say, so he cleared his throat and stood. "I was just going to check on Molly."

"I'll come with you." She stood and followed him down the steps and across the yard. As they crossed the driveway toward the barn, the moon went behind the clouds, and they were plunged into darkness. She reached for his hand. He took it automatically. She took his hand so often that it seemed almost natural now. He glanced down at their entwined hands, and she squeezed his briefly.

"Sorry, it's pretty dark, and I'll fall for sure if I don't hold your hand," she said.

"It's fine." He held her hand firmly and kept her from falling when she tripped at the entrance to the sheep shed.

He flicked on the lights. His small flock of sheep blinked sleepily from their large pen, and they walked past them to the back where the jugs were. Despite the light, they were still holding hands, but he had already decided he wasn't letting go until she did.

He looked into Molly's pen. Morgan squeezed his hand excitely. "She had her babies!"

He watched the two lambs suckling at Molly's udder. "I'm surprised she had them tonight."

"They're so sweet, so little." Morgan leaned over the pen and stared at them. "Such a good mama, Molly, feeding your babies."

They saw the little one at the same time. Morgan moaned in dismay as Gabe dropped her hand and quickly unlatched the pen. The third baby was lying still in the corner of the pen, its fur still wet and its eyes closed.

"Oh no!" Morgan followed him in, and she dropped to her knees before the tiny lamb. "Is it dead?"

He knelt beside her and rubbed the baby roughly. It was cold to the touch but twitched, and its mouth opened in a silent cry.

"We have to help it." Morgan was nearly crying. He picked up the cold baby, cradled it against his chest, and carried it out of the pen. Morgan followed him, latching the pen firmly behind her.

"Gabe? Shouldn't we give it to Molly?"

"No. She's rejected it. We need to warm it up and get some colostrum and milk into it."

He walked rapidly to the house. The dogs were sniffing

excitedly at his pants, jumping to try to smell the lamb as he walked. "Enough," he said sharply, and they quieted.

There was a thud behind him and he turned to see Morgan on her hands and knees on the ground. She scrambled to her feet, motioning him to go on. "I'm fine. Keep going."

Once they were in the kitchen, he grabbed some towels from the laundry room and handed them to Morgan. She unfolded one of them as he checked the baby's sex and then placed the lamb into the towel in her arms. "Start drying her off. Don't be too rough, but try to wipe as much of the afterbirth off her as you can."

She nodded and sat down on the floor of the kitchen. The dogs crowded around her as she began to dry the baby, and she gave them the hand command to lie down. They obeyed her immediately, and she muttered, "Good puppies," before drying the lamb.

Gabe, collecting the bottle, nipple and a large syringe from the cupboard, blinked in surprise. The dogs rarely obeyed commands from anyone but him. He opened the drawer that held the bag of powdered colostrum and the bag of powdered sheep milk. Working quickly, he mixed the colostrum with warm water and sucked it up with the syringe.

"I think she's starting to warm up," Morgan said. The lamb was moving in her lap, and she held it closer. "That's a good sign, right?"

"Yes." He sat down across from her. "Give her to me."

She handed over the baby and watched, fascinated, as he tucked it under his arm and used his hand to open its mouth. He carefully syringed the colostrum into its mouth, grunting with satisfaction when the baby swallowed it.

"She's eating it!" Morgan scooted closer and petted the lamb's back. "Is that milk?"

"No, it's colostrum. The baby needs it in the first eighteen hours or so. It has antibiotics and other important stuff in it. Normally they would get it from mom, but the powder stuff will do in a pinch. Can you make up a bottle of milk?"

"Yes." She bounded to her feet.

"Just follow the instructions on the bag. It will tell you how much powder to water ratio."

She quickly mixed the bottle as he syringed the rest of the colostrum into the lamb's mouth. She sat down next to him and handed him the bottle. He put the nipple into the lamb's mouth and waited. It didn't start to suck, and Morgan made a soft groan. "It's not eating."

"She doesn't know how to suck from a bottle. The instinct is to look for mom's nipple." He squeezed the bottle, and some milk dripped from the nipple onto the baby's tongue.

"C'mon baby, c'mon…" Morgan whispered pleadingly. She was leaning against him, her hands resting on his thigh and her hair falling over one shoulder to brush against his shirt sleeve.

He squeezed the bottle again, and more milk dripped onto the baby's tongue. It moved its mouth weakly, and Morgan inhaled sharply. Her small hands squeezed his thigh as she stared at the lamb. "Please, baby."

"If she can't figure it out, we'll syringe it into her," he reassured her.

The baby began to suck, and Morgan gave a small cry of delight. "She's doing it."

He smiled. "Yeah, she is."

She studied the lamb carefully. She was white with grey legs and a grey spot on her forehead. As Gabe continued to feed the lamb, she carefully wiped down its legs with another towel until its coat was completely dry.

"How often will we have to feed her?"

"About every two to three hours." The lamb started to tire, so he pulled the bottle from its mouth.

"Do you want me to stay here tonight? I can take a few of the night shifts," she offered.

He shook his head. It would be torture to have Morgan sleeping in the same house as him. "No, that's okay."

"I don't mind."

"You'll be tired tomorrow, and you have to go to work. I can nap during the day if need be."

"I'll come by first thing in the morning and do one of the feedings, okay?"

He nodded. "Sure."

"What should we name her?"

He gave her a cautious look. "Maybe we should wait until tomorrow. She might not make it through the night, Morgan."

She smiled at him. "She'll make it. She needs a name."

He returned her smile. "Do you have any suggestions?"

She stared at the tiny baby for a few minutes. "Lemon."

"Lemon?"

She flushed a little. "Well, she's kind of a lemon right? Is that a stupid name?"

"No. It's a good name."

Morgan petted the now-sleeping lamb and kissed the top of its head. "Sweet little Lemon – be strong, baby girl."

She sighed and stood up. "I'd better get to bed. It's getting late. I'll come by before work tomorrow, okay?"

"Okay."

She squeezed his shoulder briefly. "Good night, Gabe."

"Good night, Morgan."

* * *

Morgan glanced up at Gabe as they climbed out of his truck and started toward the backyard of his sister's place. "Okay?"

"Yeah. A little nervous," he admitted.

"It'll be fine. Lacey said it's all people you guys went to school with."

"I haven't seen most of them since high school." His side was hurting. He didn't think it was nerves. It had been painful and throbbing for over a week, and he had lost most of his appetite. He'd even thrown up this morning after breakfast. He sighed. He would have to go to the doctor, and just the thought of going was making him even more nauseous. Ever since the accident, anyone wearing a white lab coat made him want to puke.

"Are you sure you're okay, Gabe? You're pale." Morgan was frowning at him.

"I'm fine."

"If you don't want to do this, we don't have to. You know that, right?"

"I know. I – I want to," Gabe lied. He didn't want to, but he also didn't want to sit at home alone while Morgan went to the barbecue. They spent nearly every Saturday together now. He made her dinner while she did her laundry, and they usually watched a movie after dinner.

When she had brought up the barbecue, he told her he was going to Lacey's on impulse – an impulse he was now deeply regretting.

"Gabe, you're really pale and sweaty." Morgan frowned and pressed her hand on his forehead before moving it to his right and left cheek. He closed his eyes at her touch. He wasn't even thinking about the fact that she was touching his scars. He was too wrapped up in the slow burn of excitement in his belly that always happened when she touched him. It even blotted out the pain.

"I think you have a fever. Are you feeling okay?" She dropped her hand, and he had to resist the urge to follow her hand with his face, like a dog looking to be petted.

"I have a bit of a stomach ache," he admitted. "I'll ask Lacey for some Advil."

"Are you sure? Maybe we should stop at the emergency room after the barbecue and get you looked at," she said worriedly.

"No hospital. I'm fine, Morgan," he snapped at her.

"Okay." She didn't seem upset by his grumpiness, but he immediately felt bad.

"I'm sorry, I didn't mean to snap. I'm just nervous."

"I know. But it'll be fine – you'll see."

There was an excited shout, and then Natalia hurtled towards them. "Uncle Gabe!" She threw herself at him, and he caught her, wincing a little at the pain in his side before settling her in his arms.

"I didn't know you were coming tonight!"

"I wanted to surprise you, Nat." He kissed her smooth cheek, and she threw her arm around his neck.

"Hi, Ms. Wilson."

"Hello, honey. Are you enjoying your first week of summer vacation?"

"Yep. I don't miss school at all."

Morgan laughed as they walked toward Lacey and Peter. "I'll tell you a secret – I haven't started to miss it yet either."

"Where's Lemon?" Natalia asked.

"She's in the pasture with the other sheep, Nat."

"Oh." Natalia sighed in disappointment. "I thought you would bring her."

Gabe squeezed her gently. "She needs to spend time with the flock."

"I bet she would like me if she spent more time with me," Natalia said.

"Nat, you know that the lambs are skittish of humans," Gabe reminded her.

"But she loves Ms. Wilson," Natalia protested.

Gabe glanced at Morgan. It was true - Lemon did love Morgan. She followed her around the house and the yard like a dog, and if Morgan went into the pasture, Lemon immediately left the other sheep to stand next to her.

"That's because she bottle-fed her, honey. If we ever have another lamb that needs to be bottle-fed, you can help us with it okay? Then the lamb won't be afraid of you."

"Okay," the little girl agreed happily.

"So now you're turning my daughter into a sheep farmer?" Lacey raised one eyebrow at him before giving him a brief hug.

"I'm so glad you came," she whispered into his ear.

He watched as Morgan hugged Peter. A thin thread of jealousy went through him, but he was being ridiculous. Morgan didn't hug him because he had made it clear that he didn't want to be hugged.

She was a touchy-feely kind of person – that was obvious right away - and he knew she suppressed that urge when she was around him. She couldn't fully suppress it. She tended to sit too close to him when they were sitting on the couch, and she would brush her hand across his back or pat him gently on the arm when she walked by him.

He pretended not to notice, pretended that her soft touches didn't drive him crazy. They *did* drive him crazy and it was only getting worse. Sometimes, just *thinking* about her hand brushing his back would give him an erection. He knew he should ask her to stop, but at some point in the last month, the thought of her not touching him was worse than having to conceal his excitement when she did touch him. He had learned to live with his dick being half-hard every time he was around her.

He masturbated nearly every night now, picturing Morgan's sweet face, her pink lips and soft hands until he came explosively. He would lay in bed afterward with guilt coursing through him for using Morgan's attempts at friendship to fuel his schoolboy fantasies. He knew it was pointless to picture her ever joining him in his bed, but he was helpless to stop.

"Come on." Lacey tugged on his arm, startling him out of his thoughts. "Why don't you say hi to everyone?"

He took a deep breath and followed her toward the people near the patio.

CHAPTER 6

"Morgan, I can't thank you enough." Lacey hugged her impulsively as Morgan tossed a pile of paper plates into the garbage in the kitchen.

"For what?" Morgan returned her hug in bewilderment.

"What do you mean for what? For Gabe. I know you convinced him to come to the barbecue," Lacey replied.

"I didn't actually. When I said I was leaving for your place, he told me he was going too."

"Yeah, well – I know your friendship these last few months has made a difference. He seems much happier. And he let you touch him when you first arrived."

Morgan glanced at her. "What do you mean?"

"He never lets Natalia or me touch any part of his face, and you touched the scarred side like it was no big deal," Lacey said.

Morgan stared out the small window above the sink that faced the backyard. She searched for Gabe. He was standing next to the fence, and Sally Winger, a small and incredibly busty blonde, was standing beside him. Gabe said something, and Sally gave an exaggerated and breathy laugh, throwing her head back and chest out as she rested her hand on Gabe's arm.

He pulled his arm away, and Morgan could feel a smug smile on her lips. He didn't pull away when *she* touched him.

Lacey peered out the window. "Oh my God, Sally's hitting on Gabe. Look at how uncomfortable he looks – poor guy."

She laughed as she rinsed the utensils and put them in the dishwasher. "I think it's good for him, though."

Morgan didn't reply. Her stomach was twisting with what she recognized reluctantly as jealousy. It was ridiculous. She and Gabe were friends, and she wanted the best for him. If that was some stacked blonde with the IQ of a gnat, then so be it.

Unkind.

She decided that the thought probably *was* unkind, but it didn't make it any less true. She watched as Sally pressed her hand onto his arm again and felt a stronger, deeper surge of jealousy when, this time, Gabe didn't pull away.

"Morgan?"

"Hmm?"

Lacey touched her arm, and Morgan forced herself to look away from Gabe and Sally.

"I asked if you're sure you don't mind popping by the house a couple of times to check the mail and water the plants while we're gone."

"I don't mind at all. You're leaving tomorrow?"

"Yes. We were going to leave on Monday, but Peter thinks we'll miss the worst of the traffic if we leave tomorrow." She glanced around her messy kitchen. "Of course, he doesn't need to clean the kitchen, do laundry, or pack for everyone."

Morgan laughed. "How long are you gone for again?"

"Just ten days. It'll be nice to get away, though. We haven't gone camping in forever, and Natalia loves it."

Morgan's gaze drifted to Gabe and Sally again. Her hand

was still on his arm, and although he wasn't pulling free, he looked decidedly uncomfortable, and his normally tanned skin was still pale. She made a sudden decision.

"Unless you need me to stay and help clean up, I think I'm going to rescue your brother from Sally and see if he's ready to go home. I'm tired and have a bit of a headache," she fibbed.

"I don't need your help. Peter will grumble, but he'll clean up the kitchen while I'm packing. Thank you again, Morgan. I really appreciate everything you've done for Gabe. Your friendship has really helped him." Lacey hugged her.

"I'm glad he's more outgoing. Have a safe trip, and we'll talk to you when you return, okay?" Morgan said with a soft smile.

* * *

GABE, HIS HAND PRESSING AGAINST THE THROBBING PAIN IN HIS side, closed the door of the sheep shed. It was Sunday afternoon, and with the help of Vincent and Delilah, they had just herded the sheep into their pens for the night. It was early, but his side was hurting with a fierce kind of pain that radiated through his entire upper body. He wanted to have a hot shower and go to bed early. He hadn't been able to eat at all today. The toast he had eaten this morning had come right back up. He felt too warm, and he had a pounding headache.

Wincing a little, he started walking toward the house. The pain in his side increased to an almost intolerable level, and he stopped, bending over and breathing deeply. A bout of nausea overcame him, and he dry-heaved wretchedly. His stomach was empty, and nothing but a thin trickle of bile came out. He dry-heaved again, his side burning and throbbing, and for one bleak moment, he thought he would pass out from the pain.

Through the haze of pain, he felt the comforting touch of Morgan's hand on his back. "Gabe? Honey, what's wrong?"

She had come up behind him, she must have been in the barn with Daisy, and he gripped her hand so hard that she winced a little.

"Side – hurts," he said.

She felt his forehead. "Gabe, you're burning up. Come on, honey. We need to get you to the hospital."

"No!" He winced again as he straightened. "I just need to rest. I don't need the hospital."

Morgan shouted with alarm when Gabe suddenly sagged against her. His weight drove her to her knees, and she gave another cry of alarm when he crumpled to the ground.

"Gabe! Gabe! Can you hear me?"

Gabe groaned and tried to focus on her. Although she was leaning over him with her face directly above his, her voice was muffled and distant.

"Hurts," he whispered again. Vincent and Delilah paced around them, both of them whimpering low in their throats.

"Gabe! Stay awake! Don't faint on me, honey. Gabe!"

"Morgan, hurts…" Gabe's eyes rolled up in his head, and he passed out.

* * *

GABE SQUINTED AT THE UNFAMILIAR CEILING. THERE WAS A loud beeping noise, and he glanced to his left, staring in confusion at the machine. There was an IV in his hand, and he made a soft groan. He was in the hospital.

Morgan leaned over him, her hand resting on his forehead and her light blue eyes filled with worry. "How do you feel, honey?"

"Thirsty," he rasped.

"Here. It's just ice chips, but it'll help." She tipped the

Styrofoam cup, and he took some ice chips into his mouth. They began to melt, and water trickled down his dry throat.

"What happened?" he asked.

"It was your appendix. It came dangerously close to bursting. Another few hours and it would have. You should have told me how bad you were feeling," she scolded him gently.

"How long have I been out?"

"Over twenty-four hours. It's Monday night. You had emergency surgery yesterday to remove your appendix. Do you remember waking up in the recovery room? The nurses said you were quite agitated when you woke up."

He shook his head. "I don't remember."

"You were yelling and kicking up a fuss about being hospitalized. They had to give you a sedative to calm you down."

He sighed tiredly. "I don't remember any of that."

* * *

MORGAN BREATHED A SIGH OF RELIEF AT GABE'S ADMISSION. They'd allowed her to stay in his room with him last night after she lied and said she was his girlfriend. At some point, she woke from where she had dozed off in the chair to discover he was awake and staring at her. She sat on the side of the bed and stroked his blanket-covered chest as he moved restlessly.

They had given him not just a sedative but some powerful pain relief as well, and he was as high as a kite. He held her hand, fingers stroking her wrist, and told her earnestly that she was the most beautiful woman he had ever seen. He told her that he thought about kissing her every day and that he liked the way she touched him and looked at him like he wasn't hideous.

She'd blinked back tears as he sighed and muttered, "I wish I weren't ugly," before drifting back to sleep.

She was thankful he didn't remember. She'd even been flattered by what he said until she remembered he was speaking under the influence of the drugs. Still, she knew he would be mortified if he remembered what he had said to her, and she suspected he might even stop being her friend if he knew. Over the last couple of months, he had become very important to her and the thought of not being his friend filled her with dismay.

"When can I get out of here?" He asked.

She squeezed his arm. "Not for at least another day. They're giving you antibiotics through IV and want to monitor you for a bit longer."

He groaned. "I can't stay here that long. I have the sheep and Daisy and -"

She hushed him. "I went this morning and let Daisy and the sheep out to the pasture, and I just got back from putting them into the shed."

"You did that?"

She flushed a little. "Well, saying I did it might be a stretch. Vincent and Delilah did most of the work."

She giggled. "You should have seen them, Gabe. They just kept looking at me while I tried to herd the sheep. Finally, they gave each other this look that practically screamed, 'rookie' and took over. They had all the sheep in the shed in less than five minutes. Those dogs are amazing."

"You're amazing," he blurted out and then blushed.

"I am pretty awesome." She winked at him and sat in the chair beside the bed.

* * *

GABE STUDIED MORGAN CAREFULLY. SHE LOOKED TIRED, AND there were dark circles under her eyes. He frowned as a hazy memory of her hand rubbing his chest and her soft voice murmuring surfaced in his brain.

"Did you stay here last night?"

She nodded and yawned. "I did. I was worried about you. Oh, I also texted Lacey to let her know what happened. She was going to come home immediately, but I told her not to. I can help you around the farm until you're feeling better."

"You don't have to do that. I'll be able to do it."

"No, you won't, Gabe. You've still got some good pain relief coursing through your veins. Trust me – when that wears off, and all they give you is Tylenol, you'll feel much worse."

"Besides," she continued cheerfully, "I don't mind. I'm on summer holidays, remember? My days are free."

"Morgan, thank you. I -"

She suddenly sat up and cocked her head to the side. He could hear voices coming down the hall, and she leaned forward. "Listen, I told the nurses I was your girlfriend. They wouldn't have let me stay with you if I didn't. Play along, okay?"

She said the last part in a fierce little mutter as a nurse entered the room. "You're awake. How are you feeling, Mr. Dern?"

"Fine. Can I leave tonight?"

She laughed as Morgan rolled her eyes. "Your girlfriend told us you'd ask to leave when you woke up. I'm afraid you won't be going anywhere tonight. The surgeon has left for the day, and he'll want to examine you before he signs the release forms. You're stuck with us for another night."

She smiled at Morgan as she pulled back the bed covers. Her hands reached for the hospital gown, and Gabe pushed them away. "I just want to look at your incision, Mr. Dern. We don't want it getting infected."

Gabe could feel sweat breaking out on his forehead. He didn't want Morgan to see his scarred upper body. It was bad enough that she could see his left arm under the short-sleeved hospital gown.

Morgan suddenly stood. "I think I'll grab a drink and stretch my legs. Honey, are you okay with me leaving for a while?"

"Uh, yeah, that's fine, um, sweetheart." Gabe twitched in surprise when Morgan leaned over him and pressed her lips briefly against his before leaving the room.

As the nurse lifted his gown and peeled back the bandage, he stared up at the ceiling, his lips tingling and his cheeks red as he relived the firm pressure of Morgan's soft lips on his.

CHAPTER 7

"Here, let me take off your shoes." Morgan bent in the hallway of the farmhouse and tugged off his shoes.

"Okay?" She asked anxiously as she popped back up.

He nodded. "Yeah, I'm good."

"I can tell when you're lying, Gabe. Come on, let's get you into bed, and then I'll give you some pain relief meds."

They had sent him home with two morphine pills, one for this afternoon and one for this evening, and she was glad. Gabe was pale and sweaty, and she had a feeling that he was in much more pain than he would admit.

She put her arm around his waist and steadied him as he walked down the hall to his bedroom. "Where are the dogs?"

"They're with the sheep. I didn't want them in the house when I first brought you home. They'd be too excited, and I'm pretty sure they'd trip us both."

They were at his bedroom now, and she helped him inside, glancing curiously around. She had never been in his room. She'd spent more time wondering what it looked like than she cared to admit to herself.

"This is nice." She glanced at the large bed and the gas fireplace built into the opposite wall. The room was painted a dark green, which gave it a warm and cozy feel. It would be nice in the winter, she mused, although it was a bit stuffy right now. As Gabe sat gingerly on the bed, she crossed the room and opened the window, hoping to catch a breeze. It was hot out, and the farmhouse didn't have air conditioning.

"Bathroom?" She pointed to the door to her left, and he nodded.

"Do you want to use it before I tuck you into bed?"

He shook his head no, and she turned on the ceiling fan over the bed, stretching on her tiptoes to catch the cord.

"Tired?" She gave him a look of sympathy as she stood in front of him, and he nodded.

"Hold on a minute." She dug out the bottle of pills from her purse and went into the bathroom. She returned with a glass of water and held out one of the pills to him. "Here, take this."

* * *

GABE TOOK THE PILL WITHOUT ARGUMENT, DRINKING THE entire glass of water in three large gulps. The room was hot, and he could feel the sweat sticking to the back of his long-sleeved shirt. She had brought him a change of clothes to wear home from the hospital, just a pair of lightweight shorts and his usual long-sleeved shirt.

"Shorts on or off?" Morgan asked.

He blushed. "On."

There was no way he was letting her see him in his underwear. The nurses helped him dress while she got her car. Now, even with his side aching, he didn't entirely trust that he wouldn't get an erection if she took his shorts off of him.

He realized with a start that she was unbuttoning his shirt, and he grabbed at her hands, groaning with pain when it pulled at the staples in his side.

She frowned. "What?"

"I'll sleep with my shirt on."

"Don't be ridiculous. It's like a million degrees in here. You'll be much too warm."

He tried to protest again, but it was really warm in the bedroom, and the thought of trying to sleep in his shirt was unpleasant.

"I can do it," he muttered, brushing at her hands again. "I don't need your help."

"Yes, you do," she said. She finished unbuttoning his shirt, and he closed his eyes. She slipped the shirt off his shoulders and arms. He couldn't look at her. He couldn't stand to see the disgust and pity in her eyes when she saw his ravaged body for the first time.

"Holy Hannah," she breathed.

His heart dropped to his feet, and he could feel the heat rising to his cheeks. He forced himself to open his eyes.

"You've got a six pack."

He twitched a little in surprise. Morgan was staring at his abdomen. Scarring covered the left side and the muscles hidden beneath the scars, but the right side of his abs was perfect.

"How the heck do you have a six pack? You sit at a computer all day." She gave him an indignant look. "I'm constantly moving, standing, and lifting chubby little kids all day, and I don't have a six pack."

He blushed furiously as she continued. "Do you get this from working the sheep farm? Because I will take over the farm for you if it means I'll get stomach muscles like that." She reached out to trace the firm skin before snatching her hand away.

She looked up at him. "Seriously, Gabe. How did you get so muscular?"

Still blushing, he said. "I have a home gym. I work out for two hours nearly every morning."

Her face fell. "Rats. I should have known it would be from the gym."

"You don't like going to the gym?"

"Oh, I liked it. I belonged to a gym in the city. But after I fell off the treadmill for the third time and nearly broke my leg in a Zumba class, they banned me. They said they didn't have enough liability insurance to cover me. I tried going to some other gyms in the area, but they rejected me."

She frowned. "They denied it, but I'm pretty sure the other gym faxed them a picture of me with a big 'Do not admit' sign."

He laughed. The pain meds had kicked in, and he didn't wince when the staples pulled. She crouched and studied the incision on his right side. "It's looking pretty good."

"Thanks. I asked them to keep the scarring to a minimum and told them I didn't want my perfect body ruined with scars."

She gaped at him and then giggled when she realized he was making a joke.

"Let's get you into bed." She paused. "But first, I have to know. You spray tan, don't you? You wear long-sleeved shirts all the time. That tan can't be natural."

He laughed again. "No, I don't always wear my shirt. I take it off when you're not around, and I'm working outside. I tan easily. I swear."

She gave him a suspicious look. "All right, but you should know that the minute you fall asleep, I'm searching through your bathroom for hidden bottles of spray tan."

He snickered as she helped him lay back on the bed. "And Gabe – you don't have to wear your shirt around me all the time, you know that, right? We're friends. If you want to take it off, just take it off, okay?"

He nodded and closed his eyes as she pulled the sheet to his chest. "Go to sleep. I'll be in the kitchen if you need anything."

* * *

HE WOKE IN THE DARK, DISORIENTED AND NEEDING TO PEE. He took a deep breath and touched his incision. The pain meds played hell with his thought process, but he was starting to remember where he was and what was going on. He slept most of the afternoon. Morgan woke him around dinner and helped him sit up. She had made him eat some soup.

Even though it was still warm in the room and he didn't have much of an appetite, he had gamely eaten half of it before pushing it away. The meds had worn off by then, and he was feeling grumpy and out of sorts. Morgan gave him another pill and tucked him back into bed before leaving to bring the sheep in from the pasture.

He rubbed his face with his hand and glanced at the alarm clock. It was just after one in the morning, and he stared up at the ceiling, steeling himself to sit up. He hadn't tried to sit up on his own yet. Morgan had always been there to help turn him on his side and pull him into a sitting position. She was surprisingly strong for her size.

He shifted onto his side. Pain flared along his body, and he cursed loudly. Now that Morgan was back in her own house, he didn't feel the need to be as stiff-lipped about the pain. He took another deep breath and released it in a soft scream when Morgan's voice whispered in the darkness.

"Do you need some help?"

He whipped his head around as she sat up in the bed beside him. She grinned. "You scream like a girl."

"You scared the hell out of me! What are you doing in my bed?" His heart was thudding loudly in his chest, and he had damn near wet his shorts.

She slid out of the bed. She wore a long shirt, and her pale legs gleamed as she approached his side of the bed. "It's only your third night after surgery, Gabe. I wasn't going to leave you alone."

She leaned over him and slid her hand under his shoulder. "Ready?"

He nodded, and she helped him sit on the side of the bed. She walked him over to the bathroom and opened the door. "Do you need help in the bathroom?"

He shook his head immediately. "God, no."

"Okay." She rubbed his back. "I'll be right out here if you need me."

* * *

HE SIGHED AND RELAXED AGAINST THE BED. AFTER HE FINISHED in the bathroom, Morgan helped him back to bed and gave him a glass of water before tucking him back under the sheet. He half-expected her to return to her own house or, at the very least, the guest bedroom next to his room. Instead, she climbed into the bed beside him and curled up on her side.

"Are you too warm?"

He nodded. "A bit."

She reached out and pulled the sheet down to his waist. He wanted to pull the sheet up to hide his scarred body, but he had just told her he was too warm. He lay on his back and stared up at the ceiling. After a few minutes, she leaned over him, her breath warm on his face. "Go to sleep, Gabe."

"I'm trying."

"Here, turn on your side, and I'll rub your back for you."

He frowned. "No, that's okay."

"Don't be silly. It'll help. My mom always rubbed my back when I couldn't sleep." She was pushing on him, and with a soft grunt, he turned onto his left side. He inhaled sharply at the first touch of her soft hand on his back.

"Are you okay?"

"Yes."

"Just try to relax. There isn't any more of the meds from the doctor, and you can't have some Tylenol until later today."

He closed his eyes as she rubbed his back with her warm hand. She didn't shy away from the scarred side, rubbing, circling, and massaging his entire back as he stared into the darkness.

"Is it helping?" she asked.

"Yeah," he lied. His cock was as stiff as a board in his shorts, and he thanked God for the darkness. He closed his eyes and imagined what it would feel like to have her hand slide around his front. To feel her soft fingers on his stomach before they slipped under his shorts and gripped his cock. His dick jumped in his underwear, and he opened his eyes in a hurry. If he kept thinking that way, he'd come in his pants.

He squirmed a little, and she paused before rubbing his back. "Relax, Gabe. Go to sleep."

He took a deep breath. He knew he should tell her to stop touching him, he'd never fall asleep with the feel of her hand on his back, but he couldn't bring himself to ask her to stop. Her hand felt too good on his skin. He ignored his throbbing cock and curled his hands into fists. It would be a long night.

* * *

Morgan stared worriedly at Gabe. After waking up at one, he hadn't slept at all, and she didn't like how tired he looked. She made him nap in the afternoon, which perked him up a bit. But about an hour after she returned from herding the sheep into the shed, he withdrew and grew quiet.

"Gabe, is the pain really bad?" She was starting to wonder if she shouldn't call the hospital and see if she could get more morphine for him.

He shook his head. "No, it's not bad."

"You seem quiet."

"I'm just tired."

"Okay, well, let's get you tucked into bed for the night." She helped him stand and led him to his bedroom.

* * *

GABE STEPPED NERVOUSLY INTO THE BEDROOM. HE WASN'T lying when he said the pain wasn't that bad. In fact, it was much better than it had been yesterday. What worried him were the sleeping arrangements. He didn't know if Morgan was planning on sleeping in his bed again, and he wasn't sure he could stand to lay there in the darkness with her soft body next to his.

He sat on the bed and took a deep breath. "Morgan, about the sleeping arrangements, I think -"

She smiled at him. "I'm going to sleep in the guest room tonight. I have a feeling you didn't sleep well because I was in bed with you, so I'll take the guest bed and leave the doors open. If you need me at night, just holler, okay?"

He nodded, feeling relief and disappointment flood through him. "I'm sorry. I'm, uh, I'm not used to having someone else in the bed with me."

"It's fine." She gave him a cheerful smile. "I'll see you in the morning."

She squeezed his shoulder and left his bedroom.

* * *

Morgan woke a few hours later. She frowned, wondering what had woken her until she heard Gabe's low voice crying out in the darkness. She was out of bed and running into his room before she was fully awake.

Gabe was lying on his side. His hands were clenched into fists, and he was moaning loudly. She climbed onto the bed beside him and rested her hand on his shoulder.

"Gabe? Honey, wake up."

He continued to moan, and she flicked on the bedside lamp. His face was contorted with pain and fear, and her heart constricted in response. "Honey, wake up now."

"Tony?" He frowned in his sleep, and the confusion and fear in his voice sent chills down her spine. "Watch out, Tony!"

He shuddered and twitched. "I can't get out – I can't – someone help me!" He gave a loud cry, and his entire body heaved.

"Gabe!" Her fear for him made her rough as she shook his shoulder. "Baby, open your eyes."

"It hurts! Oh God, it hurts so much. Please help me…"

His voice trailed off into a quiet little moan, and she shook him again.

"Wake up, Gabe! Wake up right now!" Adrenaline flooded her body, making her limbs tremble and her heart pound.

Gabe's eyes popped open, and she took his hand in hers. "Hi, honey. You're okay, do you hear me?"

His hand squeezed down on hers so tightly she had to bite back her cry of pain. He stared at her wild-eyed, his body shaking and his skin covered in sweat. His face was ashen, and his mouth was trembling.

"Morgan?"

"Yeah, sweetie. It's Morgan. You're okay." He continued to

79

shake, and unable to stand it, she laid down beside him and pulled him into her embrace. He tucked his face into the curve of her neck and shuddered as she rubbed his back.

"It was just a bad dream, baby. You're okay, shh," she whispered into his ear. She stroked the back of his head, threading her fingers through his thick hair.

After a few moments, he raised his head and stared at her. "I'm sorry."

"You have nothing to be sorry about." She kissed his fore-head and then his cheeks. He took a deep shuddering breath, and she pressed her mouth against his. He stiffened against her, and she pressed light kisses against his mouth.

"You're okay, honey," she whispered against his mouth before kissing him again.

He moaned and twitched at the first feel of her tongue stroking his lips. He hesitated and then opened his mouth, and she immediately slipped her tongue into his mouth. She ran it over his teeth before plunging it deep into his mouth. She rubbed her tongue along his and pressed her soft body against his. He put his hands tentatively around her waist as she rubbed her breasts against his hard chest.

She moaned her encouragement, and her tongue curled against his, urging it into her mouth. He pushed it into her mouth, tasting her sweetness as she ran her hands over his chest.

She trembled against him as he tasted her. She had only wanted to comfort him, to make him feel better after his nightmare, but what started as comforting had quickly turned into something else. Her pelvis throbbed with need, and her nipples were hard and tight. The soft material of her sleep shirt irritated them, and she wanted to pull off her shirt and press her nipples against Gabe's naked chest.

He was kissing her with a determined sort of awkward-ness, and she wondered about his timidity as he brushed his hands against her ribs but didn't move them higher to her aching breasts. She wanted him – he had to know that.

He wanted her too - she could feel his erection pushing against her belly. She ground her hips against him, and he moaned into her mouth.

She gripped his arms and fell onto her back on the bed, pulling him with her. He made a low moan of pain, and his hand pressed against his side even as he continued to kiss her eagerly.

She immediately pulled her mouth away and pushed him gently onto his back. She quickly checked his incision. It looked okay, and she shoved her hair out of her eyes before giving him a horrified look. "Gabe, I'm sorry."

* * *

SHAME FLOODED THROUGH GABE. HE TORE HIS GAZE FROM hers and stared at the ceiling, panting harshly as his hands clenched and unclenched at his sides.

"I'm sorry," she repeated herself. "I shouldn't have done that."

He jerked and winced again. "It's fine." He turned his face away from her and reached for the sheets, flinching as he pulled them up to his neck. He knew she could see the outline of his erection against the sheet.

"Gabe? Are you okay?"

He nodded. "I'm fine. You should go back to the guest room. I'm really tired, and my side is aching."

She slid from the bed. "Of course. I – I'm sorry, Gabe."

She nearly ran from the room, and Gabe stared blankly at the ceiling. What just happened was the most incredible moment of his life until she pulled away. He'd seen the look on her face when she realized what she was doing, and the dim light did nothing to hide the horrified look on her face.

81

She'd had a moment of insanity, and she had pushed him away when she realized what she was doing. His gut clenched in misery. It was stupid to think that Morgan could ever be attracted to him.

He was a monster.

CHAPTER 8

Morgan sighed and leaned against Daisy's solid warmth. She could feel tears wanting to leak down her face, and she held them back grimly. Today had been terrible. She thought that she would explain to Gabe that she stopped last night because she hurt him. She had been so eager to ease her own need for him that she hadn't even thought about the fact that he was recovering from surgery. And it wasn't just that. He'd had a terrible nightmare, and she had basically attacked him.

She straightened and started to brush Daisy again. Gabe refused to speak to her about it, and there was a coldness to him that she hadn't seen since the first few days she knew him. She had torn down his walls with patience and friendship and, in one stupid night, hurt him so badly that he built them back up even stronger and higher than when she first met him.

She thought he wanted her. His kisses were tentative, and there was a weird awkwardness about them, but his cock had been hard and heavy against her. During the long, sleepless night, she decided he was awkward because his side hurt. But then there was his coldness to her all day, and she came to a different conclusion.

He'd been confused and disoriented from his nightmare. He was looking for a comforting touch, and she provided one until she started mauling him like some horny teenage girl. He responded the way he did because she left him no choice.

She sighed and left Daisy's stall, latching it firmly before heading out of the barn. She would talk to Gabe and make him listen to her when she apologized again for last night. He couldn't avoid her forever. He still needed her help.

She frowned. There was a car in the driveway that she didn't recognize. Feeling weirdly uneasy, she hurried to the house and let herself in the back door. There was a cloyingly sweet smell of lavender in the air, and she followed it to the living room.

"Gabe? Are you -"

She stopped in the doorway. Gabe sat on the couch wearing track pants and a long-sleeved shirt, and Sally sat next to him, her hand resting on his leg.

"Oh, hi, Morgan!" Sally smiled at her.

"Um, hi, Sally. What, uh, what are you doing here?"

"I heard about Gabe's surgery, and I thought I should come by and check on him. I know that Lacey is out of town, and I was worried about our little Gabriel."

"That's nice of you," Morgan said. "But I've been helping Gabe and -"

"Oh, I know! Gabe told me how you've been caring for him and the animals. I'm so impressed. I wouldn't have a clue how to herd sheep." She smiled at Gabe and squeezed his leg. "Maybe when you're feeling better, you could teach me?"

"Uh – sure, I guess." Gabe's face was bright red, and he gave Sally a thin smile.

Sally shifted, and the smell of her perfume wafted to

Morgan once more. She was painfully aware of her own smell. She had been cleaning the stall and knew she smelled like a combination of Daisy and manure.

"Did you know you have dirt on your face, Morgan?" Sally asked.

Morgan flushed. "Yeah, I was cleaning out Daisy's stall."

"How nice." Sally smiled again at her. "Anyway, I thought I would help you and Gabe out. I'm sure you're very busy and -"

"I'm not," Morgan said. "I'm on summer holidays."

"Oh, of course. I meant that you were probably busy with all the chores around the farm and helping Gabe around the house. I came by to offer my babysitting services in the evening."

"Babysitting services?" Morgan raised one eyebrow at her.

Sally laughed, a tinkling little girl laugh that set Morgan's teeth on edge. "You know what I mean."

Morgan glanced at Gabe. He was staring at the floor, his face red and sweaty, and he looked so miserable and uncomfortable that she felt a grudging sympathy for him.

"I've just told Gabe that I'm more than happy to stop by every evening and cook him dinner and keep him company. Help him bathe, do his laundry, or whatever he needs to help him get back on his feet."

"Again, that's very kind of you, but we've managed just fine." Morgan's patience was wearing thin.

Sally gave her a brittle smile. "Why don't we let Gabe decide if he'd like my help? He is a grown man, after all."

Morgan flushed again. "Of course."

Sally rubbed the top of Gabe's leg. "Gabe, sweetie, do you want me to pop by in the evenings to help you?"

Gabe cleared his throat. "Sure. I appreciate your offering to help out. That's real, um, neighbourly of you."

Morgan tried to hide her shock and hurt when he quickly glanced at her.

Sally clapped her hands together. "Great! You stay right here, and I'll get started on dinner. I make a mean chicken casserole." She stood and smiled at Morgan. "Will you be joining us for dinner, Morgan?"

"No," Morgan said.

"Well, you have a good evening then."

"You too." She left the living room without looking at Gabe.

* * *

GABE SIGHED MISERABLY AS HE STARED AT THE LASAGNA ON HIS plate. Beside him, Sally chattered on, telling him about her day as she sipped at her glass of wine and ate tiny nibbles of lasagna.

It had been the longest three days of his life. He'd accepted Sally's offer for help and regretted it immediately. He was desperate to think of a way to keep Morgan away from him, and accepting Sally's help seemed like the thing to do.

Not that it hadn't worked to keep Morgan away. It *had* worked – too well. Morgan stopped in briefly each morning and again at lunch to check on him, and that was it. She stood in the hallway, avoiding his gaze and keeping her slender arms wrapped around herself. Every evening at six, Sally showed up and spent the evening with him. He had grown tired of her after the first night. She talked non-stop, filled with nothing but gossip about people he barely knew and cared even less about.

She had a nervous energy about her that made *him* nervous, and more than once, he caught her staring at his face with a look of pity in her eyes. It irritated him, especially after weeks of Morgan's calm presence and her genuine ability to not even notice his scars.

He knew Morgan was taking excellent care of the animals. He watched from the window as she brought the sheep and Daisy out each morning and herded them back in every night. She had quickly caught on to the rhythm of Vincent and Delilah's herding, and the three of them were an efficient team.

He missed her. He missed her laugh and how she gently teased him. He missed her soft touches and how her eyes danced in the light.

"Gabe? Hello, Gabe?"

He looked up from his untouched plate of food. "Sorry, what was that?"

"I asked if you're sure you don't want me to spend the night. You know I don't mind." Sally smiled at him, her eyes skittering away from the left side of his face. He turned to face her fully, taking an odd perverse pleasure in the way she smiled nervously when presented with the blasted skin of his left side.

"I'm sure," he said. "In fact, I think I'm doing much better, and I probably don't need -"

"You can't push yourself, Gabe," Sally said. "You think you're doing better, but it hasn't even been a week. Trust me, you still need someone looking after you."

She pushed Vincent away from her pants with a look of distaste. Gabe whistled softly, and the dog joined Delilah, lying at his feet. She stood and cleared the dishes from the table.

"You hardly ate any of your supper," she scolded him. "You'll wither away, Gabriel Dern."

He didn't reply, and she squeezed his shoulder, pretending not to notice when he pulled away. "I'll do the dishes, and then we'll watch some TV."

* * *

"Thanks again, Sally. Have a good night." Gabe stood on the back porch and stared across the yard. He knew Morgan was on the porch of the carriage house. He could see the glowing ember of her cigarette.

"Are you sure you don't want me to stay, Gabe? I really don't mind." Sally pouted.

"I'm sure." He glanced at the carriage house again, wondering if she could hear them talking. He watched the small light flicker in the darkness and felt a surge of guilt. She was smoking because of him.

He realized with sudden horror that Sally was standing right next to him, too close to him, and he wrenched away from her when she slid her arms around his waist. He hissed a little at the pain that went through his side. It was the first time it had hurt today, and it reminded him of the first two days at home when it was just him and Morgan in the house. Her soft touch had soothed him in a way that Sally's never would.

Sally frowned at him. "I'm sorry."

"It's fine. Goodnight, Sally," he replied.

"Goodnight. Listen, I thought I would pop by tomorrow afternoon. It's Sunday, and I don't have to work, so I'll make you lunch, and then we'll go for a drive. It would be good for you to get out of the house."

She walked down the stairs before he could say no and slipped across the yard into her car. After another glance at the carriage house, he sighed harshly and returned to his lonely house.

* * *

MORGAN WAS TRYING NOT TO BE CRANKY. IT WAS SUNDAY afternoon, and she'd decided to stop feeling sorry for herself. So what if Gabe wasn't into her like she was into him? She was crossing the yard when Sally pulled into the driveway. The smaller woman climbed out of the car. She started to speak, but Morgan just waved and hurried towards the barn. She had no desire to talk to the busty blonde.

She entered the barn, inhaling the sweet smell of hay and Daisy's unique smell. The cow was out in the pasture with the sheep, and she opened the stall. She would give the stall a good cleaning. By the time she was done, Gabriel would be gone on his stupid drive with Busty McGee.

She sighed angrily and picked up the shovel. She had overheard them talking last night, and although it made her a horrible person, she was happy when she watched Sally going in for the kiss and Gabe pulling away from her. It made her feel slightly better that it wasn't just her that he didn't want to touch him intimately.

"Hey, Morgan."

She jumped and whirled around. Gabe was standing in the empty stall next to Daisy's.

"What are you doing in here?" She scowled at him.

"It's my barn."

"Yeah," she muttered. She pulled on her gloves and started shoveling out the stall, dumping the hay and manure into a large garbage can she had dragged over.

"Thank you for doing that. I know it's not pleasant work," he said.

"I don't mind it. Besides, you bought Daisy because I wanted her." She continued to shovel and, without looking at him, said, "Sally is here."

"I know." He made no move to leave, and she frowned at him as understanding dawned.

"You're hiding from her."

89

He blushed, and she raised her eyebrows. "Are you kidding me? You're the one who agreed to have her babysit you each night."

"Yeah, I know," he sighed. "I don't want to go for a drive."

"Then just tell her that."

"I've tried. She doesn't really understand the word no."

She rolled her eyes. "Maybe it's because she never shuts up. She just doesn't hear it."

He grinned, and she could feel an answering smile on her lips. She tamped it down fiercely.

"She does talk a lot," he said.

Delilah suddenly barked, and Gabe's eyes widened when he heard Sally's voice. "Stop jumping on me, you nasty old thing."

"Here she comes." Morgan grinned at him.

He looked around frantically for a hiding spot. "Don't tell her I'm here. Please," he whispered before ducking out of sight in the stall.

The barn door opened, and Sally walked in, her nose wrinkling at the smell.

"Morgan, have you seen Gabe?"

"As a matter of fact, he is currently cowering in the stall behind me," Morgan said cheerfully.

Sally hesitated and then gave her a strained smile. "You're funny, Morgan."

"Thanks."

"Seriously, though – we're supposed to have lunch and go for a drive."

"He must have forgotten. He went to the auction today."

"His truck is still in the driveway."

"His friend Ray picked him up. They won't be back until later tonight," Morgan lied breezily.

She threw a shovelful of manure and hay into the garbage bin. "Do you want me to give him a message?"

Sally shook her head. "No, I'll come by tomorrow night. Have a nice day, Morgan."

"You too, Sally."

She waited until she heard the sound of Sally's car pulling out of the driveway and then said, "She's gone, Braveheart. You can come out now."

Gabe didn't reply, and she frowned. "Gabe?"

Her pulse sped up when there was still no response, and she dropped the shovel and took off her gloves. She walked to the other stall and peered in. Gabe was lying on his back in the stall, his hand pressing against his side, and she crouched beside him.

"Gabe? Are you okay?" She placed her hand on his forehead, searching for the return of a fever that would indicate infection. "Gabe?"

His eyes popped open, and he grinned at her. "Boo."

She shrieked with surprise and skittered backward, falling hard on her ass and smacking her head on the hard ground of the stall.

She groaned, and Gabe's worried face appeared above her. "Morgan! Are you okay? I'm sorry!"

"You jerk!" She whacked him hard on the chest, and he winced a little.

"I'm sorry."

"I thought you had hurt your side again." She glared at him.

"I was just paying you back for your little stunt with Sally." He grinned at her as his warm breath washed over her.

She scowled. "I suppose I deserved it."

"Are you okay?" His grin faded. "I didn't mean for you to get hurt."

"I'm fine." Her gaze dropped to his mouth. His body was touching hers lightly, and her traitorous nipples were hardening and straining against her bra.

His eyes darkened, and he stared at *her* mouth for a long moment. She swallowed and licked her lips. He groaned quietly, and then his mouth was on hers, his tongue probing at her lips. She opened them, and he pushed his way into her mouth, his tongue exploring the sweet, familiar warmth.

* * *

HE SHOULDN'T BE KISSING MORGAN, BUT HE COULDN'T HELP it. He needed her with an aching fierceness that was driving him crazy. She moaned into his mouth, the sweetest sound he had ever heard, and he kissed her more deeply. She wrapped her arms around his neck and clung to him as he pressed his hard body against hers. He groaned, his hands stroking her ribs and arms repeatedly. She grabbed his hand and pushed it under her shirt.

"Touch me, Gabe," she begged against his mouth. "Please."

He hesitated and then slid his hand across the smooth skin of her stomach before cupping her breast gingerly through her bra. She moaned encouragingly and arched her upper body, pushing more of her breast into his hand.

He squeezed her breast lightly, then roughly, staring worriedly at her. "Is that – does that feel good?"

"Yes," she moaned. She shivered when he rubbed his thumb over her nipple. It was very hard, and he plucked at it through the soft cotton of her bra.

"Oh God." She shuddered and put her hands under his shirt, rubbing his hard chest for a moment before she traced his stomach with her fingers. He kissed her neck, tasting and licking the soft skin, and she angled her chin up to give him better access. He buried his face in her throat and then kissed his way to her ear, licking and sucking on her earlobe until she was moaning and twisting under him.

Growing bolder, he worked his hand under the cup of her

bra. He was desperate to feel her bare nipple, and he was so focused on it that he didn't realize she was wiggling her hand under the waistband of his shorts.

She slid her hand inside his underwear and gripped him just as he got his hand under her bra and felt her nipple pebbling against his palm. He cried out, his back arching when her hand wrapped around his cock. There was pain in his side, but it was distant and unimportant.

She stroked him firmly. Her soft hand felt unbelievably amazing on his cock as her nipple tightened against his palm. She stroked him twice more, and he could feel his groin tightening. He tried to hold back, tried to stop the orgasm rushing through him, but the combination of her hard nipple against his palm and her soft hand touching his cock made it impossible.

He climaxed with a loud shout, his hips pumping against her hand as he came all over her hand and the front of his underwear. He had barely caught his breath when embarrassment flooded through him. He stared down at her, groaning at the look of surprise on her face. He pulled his hand free of her bra and shirt and wrenched her hand out of his shorts. He scrambled to his feet, wincing a little at the pain in his side.

She sat up. "Gabe..."

"I'm sorry." His face was bright red, and he couldn't look at her. "I'm so sorry, Morgan."

He turned and ran out of the barn.

CHAPTER 9

G abe wiped the steam off the bathroom mirror and stared at the scorched landscape of his upper body. It really was hideous. He leaned forward and ran his fingers over his face. He traced the missing half of his eyebrow before running his fingers down his cheek and neck.

He left the bathroom abruptly and dressed. He had avoided Morgan for three days. He'd locked the farmhouse door so she couldn't let herself in, and he had hidden like a little kid in the kitchen when she knocked on his door a couple of times.

On the third day, he could hear the frustration in her voice when she shouted through the door. "Gabe, this is ridiculous! You have to come out of that darn house some-time. Just talk to me - please."

That night, when Sally showed up after work, he finally found his damn courage and told her that while he appreci-ated her help, he was doing fine and didn't need her to drop by anymore. She was surprised but accepted it, and he panicked a little when she invited him to her house for dinner on the weekend. He mumbled some excuse, and she gave him a watery smile and made him promise to call her at least on the weekend. He agreed hastily while steering her towards the door.

Once she was gone, he had given himself a pep talk, swallowed his pride, and walked to the carriage house. Morgan was sitting on the porch smoking a cigarette, and he had eased into the chair beside her.

"Hi, Morgan."

"Oh, so you're talking to me now?"

"Yes. I came here to apologize for what happened in the barn. Our friendship is important to me, and I don't want to ruin it."

"And you think what happened in the barn will ruin it?" She tapped the long grey ash on her cigarette into the ashtray.

"Yeah, I guess I do." He stared down at his hands, partly because he was too embarrassed to look her in the eye and partly because he might try to kiss her if he looked at her. Kissing her was a very bad idea. He had humiliated himself enough.

"It's already awkward between us. I want it to return to how it was," he lied.

If she refused and said she wanted more, he would do whatever she asked. He hated the thought of her looking at his ruined flesh, of touching it with her soft fingers and seeing the ugliness up close, but he also wanted her in his bed on a level that was close to desperation.

She sighed. "That's fine. I want that, too. It's my fault anyway. It's been a long time since I – I've been with anyone, and maybe Andy dumping me brought my self-confidence down. I guess I just needed to feel wanted, and I took advantage of you. I'm sorry, Gabriel."

He glanced at her quickly, but she stared out at the garden, the cigarette between her fingers forgotten. He swallowed the disappointment rising in his throat. She was just lonely. She had kissed him and touched him not because she wanted him but because she was lonely. She didn't see his scars like other people did, but that didn't mean she didn't notice them at all.

Or maybe it wasn't the scars at all that turned her off. Maybe it was his humiliating lack of self-control. He thought back to the way he had come all over her hand after only a few seconds of petting, and his cheeks flamed. There was a good possibility that he would never be able to look her in the eye again, no matter how hard he tried.

"Do you want to have supper at my place tomorrow night?" he asked.

"Will Sally be there?"

"No. I told her I didn't need her help anymore."

"Then yes, I'll have dinner with you." She butted her cigarette and stood up. She crossed before him, and he waited to see if she would touch his shoulder like she normally did. She didn't, and he released his breath in a soft, disappointed rush.

"Good night, Gabe. I'll see you tomorrow."

"Good night, Morgan."

Now, as he left his bedroom and headed into the kitchen, he rubbed his forehead. It had been a few days, and things were better between them, but there was still an awkwardness that neither could overcome. Worse than the awkwardness was how she no longer touched him. Not even the small brushes of her arm against his or the light touch of her hand on his back. He hadn't realized how accustomed he'd grown to her touching him until she no longer did.

He poured himself a cup of coffee as the screen door to the kitchen banged open. Expecting Morgan, he turned and smiled when Natalia came barrelling in.

"Hi, Uncle Gabe. How do you feel today?"

"I feel good, Nat. What are you doing here?"

"Mama and I are going to the farmer's market, and we stopped to see if Ms. Wilson wants to go with us."

"That's nice," Gabe said.

"Do you want to come with us?"

"Not today, Nat. I have to work."

Her face fell, and he ruffled her hair. "Why don't we go to the pasture and visit Lemon before you leave?"

"Okay!" Natalia grinned at him, and he ruffled her hair again before following her out of the kitchen.

* * *

"Morgan?" There was a soft knock on the front door and Lacey stuck her head in.

"I'm in the kitchen," Morgan called.

Lacey walked into the kitchen. "Hey, what's going on?"

"Not much. How about you?"

"Natalia and I are going to the farmer's market. Do you want to come?"

"I'd love to." Morgan drank the last of her coffee and rinsed the cup before putting it in the dishwasher.

"Natalia went to find Gabe. She wants him to go, too."

"Oh yeah?"

Lacey frowned. "Morgan, did something happen between you and Gabe while we were gone?"

"What do you mean?" Morgan tried not to noticeably tense.

"You guys don't seem as close as you were. Last night at dinner, things seemed strained between you."

Morgan shook her head. "No, everything's fine with us."

"Are you sure?"

"Positive." Morgan made herself smile at Lacey. "I forgot

to say thanks for inviting me to your family dinner, by the way."

"After everything you've done for Gabe - you're family now," Lacey replied.

Morgan's stomach twisted with guilt. She had done things to Gabe all right - things that had embarrassed him and made him feel bad. She sighed and wiped the counter with the dishcloth. She didn't know how long she could continue lying to herself and Gabe.

When he had come to her a few nights ago and told her he wanted things to return to how they were, she hastily agreed and made up her own reasons for what had happened in the barn. It was pure instinct. Afraid of losing him completely, she lied about being lonely and hurt by Andy.

If he knew the truth – if he knew that every part of her ached to touch him and be touched by him - he would withdraw completely. She had seen it on his face. She didn't know if it was because, despite what had happened between them in the barn, he really wasn't interested in her as anything more than a friend or if he would never believe that a woman could truly be attracted to him. In the end, she didn't care. She just didn't want to lose him.

"Do you know if Sally has been by lately?" Lacey asked.

"No, she hasn't been."

Lacey sighed and clasped her hands together. "I was afraid of that. Sally texted me and said she was helping to look after Gabe while he was recovering from surgery, and I hoped that maybe, you know…"

Morgan stared at her, and Lacey flushed a little. "Sally is interested in him despite his scars, and I want Gabe to have someone in his life. Someone who makes him happy, you know? I was afraid he might drive her away, and it seems he has."

She stared at the top of the table. "Poor Gabe. He's never

even had a girlfriend, and I thought that Sally being inter-ested in him might -"

"What did you say?"

"What?"

"Did you say that Gabe has never had a girlfriend?" Morgan asked.

Lacey nodded. "Yes. He was only fifteen when the acci-dent happened, and after that, he just cut himself off from everyone. He hated the way he looked."

Morgan stared at the sink. Understanding was dawning within her, and she gripped the edge of the countertop.

Gabe had never had a girlfriend.

He was a virgin.

She took a deep breath. That certainly explained things. The way he had so sweetly but awkwardly kissed her in his bed. His tentative touch in the barn and his immediate and explosive reaction when she touched his cock.

She cursed herself in her head. She should have figured it out. She knew Gabe was a teenager when the car accident happened, and she knew he was a recluse. She expected to pity him, but the thoughts coursing through her mind were of the sweeter and dirtier kind. She could almost see herself teaching Gabe everything he needed to know about love-making and showing him how good they could make each other feel.

The crotch of her panties was suddenly damp, and she bit at her lip. She had told Gabe she wouldn't touch him, had promised him they would be just friends, and knowing he had never been with a woman didn't change any of that.

"Morgan? What's wrong?" Lacey was staring at her worriedly, and Morgan smiled at her.

"Nothing's wrong." She wasn't about to confess that she wanted to seduce and deflower Lacey's brother. They were friends, but that was a hell of a thing to blurt out.

"Let me change my shirt, and I'll be ready to go." She gave Lacey another smile and left the kitchen.

* * *

MORGAN STARED WORRIEDLY AT THE SKY. IT WAS OMINOUSLY dark and big, fat raindrops were starting to fall. A summer storm, a doozy by the looks of it, was beginning, and the sheep were still out in the pasture.

Gabe had left early this morning to help Peter put a new roof on their greenhouse, and although it was after dinner, he still wasn't back. As the rain fell, she grabbed her sweater and ran out the door. The sheep and Daisy needed to be brought in.

She sprinted across the driveway and past the barn and sheep shed, ducking her head against the rain and the heavy wind. She was wearing shorts and sandals, and her feet were soaking wet and freezing.

She opened the gate to the pasture and whistled for the dogs. They loped out of the growing darkness and whined eagerly at her.

"C'mon, puppies, time to bring the sheep in." Most of the sheep had already started to crowd up towards the shed. She first brought Daisy to the smaller barn and locked her securely in her stall before heading back into the pouring rain. The water was dripping from her nose and cheeks, and she shivered miserably as, with Vincent and Delilah's help, she herded the sheep into the shed.

She closed the shed door, blocking the sound of the wind and the thunder, and breathed a sigh of relief. Vincent and Delilah crowded around her, wetting her already soaked legs with more water from their thick fur. They whined nervously, and Vincent looked at the shed door and growled deep in his chest. The fur on his neck stood up, and she patted him, trying to soothe him. The storm was making everyone jumpy and nervous. She frowned and eyed the flock of nervous animals. Lemon was missing.

"What the heck?" She looked again, her heart dropping when she couldn't see Lemon's soft white body anywhere. The ewe had grown quite a bit in the last couple of months, but she was still very much a baby and Morgan's baby at that. Her heart pounding, she turned and ran back to the pasture, closing the shed door behind her.

"Lemon!" She called for the sheep as she ran through the short grass.

Where could she be?

She squinted through the rain as the wind blew her wet hair from her face.

"Lemon, honey, where are you?" She strained to hear over the wind. She thought she heard Lemon's familiar bleating. It might have come from the left, near the grove of trees that grew at the far end of the pasture.

She quickly hiked to the trees. She could just make out Lemon's white coat against the bark of the largest tree, and she breathed a sigh of relief as she ran over to the ewe and petted her soft head.

"Lemon, you scared me half to death. Why didn't you come in with the other sheep?" She realized that the young ewe was trembling all over and bleating repeatedly.

"Lemon? What's wrong?" She ran her hands down the ewe's body, trying to stop her trembling. "Is the storm scaring you? Come on, honey, follow Mama."

The ewe stood where she was, her dark eyes large and frightened, and Morgan made a soft, soothing noise. "It's okay, Lemon. Let's go before it -"

She heard a low growling behind her, and the hair on the back of her neck tried to stand up. Her body trembling like a live wire, Morgan turned around slowly. Two large coyotes stood less than ten feet away, and her heart began pounding fiercely.

As adrenaline sang through her veins, Morgan backed up until she pressed Lemon against the tree. The coyotes stepped forward on stiff legs. Their heads were down, and their growling was getting louder.

She took a deep breath and screamed as loud as she could, clapping her hands and stomping her feet, hoping it would scare them away. They flinched and shied back but didn't run away.

Morgan screamed again as Lemon bleated behind her. She knew she could back away toward the shed, the coyotes would go after Lemon, but there was no way in hell she was leaving Lemon to be torn apart. She searched the ground for a branch or a rock, anything she could use as a weapon, as the coyotes crept forward.

* * *

Gabe cursed under his breath as he pulled into the driveway. It took him longer to get home than he anticipated. The storm was much worse in town, and the wind had knocked over a large tree. It had blocked the road, and he'd been forced to turn around and double back before taking a different route, which added an extra hour to his drive.

By the time he got to the farm, the storm was in full force, and he had to push to close the truck door against the fiercely-blowing wind. As he ran toward the sheep shed, the rain soaked him to the bone. He could hear the dogs barking, so he yanked open the shed door and stepped inside.

The sheep were in their pens, Morgan must have brought them in, and he petted Delilah absentmindedly when she crowded up to him, whining softly. Vincent stood at the other door that led to the pasture, his body stiff and his fur standing straight up. He had stopped barking but was growling and snarling at the closed door.

Gabe frowned. What was going on? Morgan had brought the sheep in, but why had she left the dogs in the shed instead of taking them to the house? And what the hell was wrong with Vincent?

He crossed the shed and stared down at the trembling dog. "Vincent, what's wrong?"

The dog barked sharply at him and pawed at the shed door. Gabe opened the door, and the dog shot out into the pasture and disappeared into the dark.

"Vincent, come!" Gabe shouted, but the dog didn't return. "What the hell?"

His blood ran cold when he heard her scream. It was faint, and he wouldn't have heard it if the wind hadn't been blowing in the right direction. He froze for half a second and then grabbed the rifle on hooks above the shed door.

Delilah came charging over, and he shouted at her to stay before slamming the door shut and running toward Vincent, who had disappeared. He was halfway across the pasture when Morgan screamed again. It had come from the grove of trees. He was sure of it. His pulse throbbing and his stomach rolling with fear, he raced toward the trees.

* * *

MORGAN COULDN'T FIND A SINGLE BRANCH OR LARGE ROCK TO use as a weapon, and she could feel the panic nipping at her as the coyotes advanced. She pressed harder against Lemon. The ewe made a strangled bleating noise but didn't squirm away. It was frozen with fear.

Morgan moaned when the coyote on the left crouched. She reached for the ewe. Fear made her desperate, and she had the wild idea of picking up Lemon and running for it.

The coyote leaped before she could even lift the ewe from the ground. Something came out of the darkness, something dark and wet and growling ferociously. Her frightened mind had just enough time to register that it was Vincent before he hit the coyote mid-leap. They tumbled to the ground, snarling and snapping at each other, and she cried out when she heard Vincent make a sharp howl of pain.

"Vincent!" Crying and shaking, she realized with horror that the other coyote was still slinking towards them. It ignored its pack mate twisting and writhing on the ground with Vincent. Its yellow eyes stared hungrily at the ewe behind her, and Morgan wrapped her arms around Lemon's thick waist.

She heaved the ewe up, her arms shaking with the weight, and took two steps forward. Her sandals slid on the wet grass, and she fell backwards on to her ass, Lemon bleating with terror as she fell on top of Morgan.

Morgan watched in horror as the coyote ran toward them. She jerked and shrieked in surprise when a loud shot rang out. The coyote collapsed to the ground only a few feet from where she was lying on the wet ground. She started to cry when she saw Gabe grimly lowering the rifle.

The second coyote, frightened by the gunshot, tore free of Vincent. Vincent staggered forward and then collapsed to the ground as the coyote barked once and turned to run. Gabe raised the rifle to his shoulder, and Morgan buried her face in Lemon's soft wool as a second shot rang out.

She cried out when Lemon was jerked away from her, but it was only Gabe. He knelt beside her and cupped her face. "Morgan! Honey, are you okay? Are you hurt?"

"No, I'm fine," she gasped out. "Vincent. Check on Vincent!"

He hesitated, and she clawed at his shirt. "Gabe, go! Please!"

He turned and ran toward Vincent as she staggered to her feet and followed him. She dropped to her knees beside Vincent's still body.

"Oh no – oh please! Gabe is he – is he dead?" She started to weep as she touched Vincent's wet fur.

Gabe shook his head. "No, but we need to get him to the vet." He lifted Vincent into his arms and strode towards the barn. Her hands shaking and rain mixing with the tears on her face, Morgan grabbed his rifle and followed him, Lemon trailing behind her.

CHAPTER 10

G abe parked the truck in the driveway and shut it off before sliding out. He crossed in front of the truck, the wind blowing his dark hair, and opened Morgan's door. She stared dully at his offered hand before taking it, and she didn't object when he led her to the farmhouse instead of the carriage house.

He sat her down at the table and turned on the kettle. "I'll make you some tea, okay?"

She didn't reply, and he frowned when she stood and paced back and forth in the small kitchen. Her face was pale, and although their clothes had mostly dried while they waited in the vet clinic, he could see her entire body shaking wildly.

He took her arm and pulled her to a stop. She stared up at him blankly, her eyes rimmed with red from crying.

"Morgan, I -"

"Please, Gabe," she whispered.

He pulled her into his embrace. She wrapped her arms around his waist and hugged him fiercely, burying her face in his damp t-shirt as she started to cry again.

"Honey, don't cry. Vincent's going to be okay. He made it through the surgery just fine."

"He saved my life, Gabe. We shouldn't have left him there," she whimpered.

He stroked her soft hair. "The vet will monitor him overnight and Delilah is with him. It's better for him to stay in the clinic where the vet and his staff can watch him."

He tipped her chin up and brushed away the tears with gentle fingers. "Are you okay? You haven't stopped shaking once."

She took a deep breath. "Yeah, I was just so scared and didn't know what to do. I couldn't leave Lemon. I just couldn't."

"I know, honey." He hugged her again, rubbing her back through her shirt, and she leaned her head against his chest. The clock said it was only ten, but it felt much later. He kissed the top of her head. "Are you hungry?"

She shook her head no and snuggled closer to his solid warmth.

"I'll make you some tea."

"I don't want tea." She stared up at him, and he swallowed thickly.

"I'll walk you back to your house."

"I don't want to be alone tonight, Gabe," she murmured. "Please don't send me away."

His heart sped up as he stared down at her sweet face. "I won't. You can stay here tonight."

"In the guest room?" she asked.

"If that's what you want."

"It isn't." She pressed herself against him, burying her face in his chest as she stroked his back.

He tried to move his pelvis away casually. His lack of self-control had reared its ugly head, and despite his best efforts to control it, his cock was reacting to her closeness. She made a soft noise in the back of her throat and pressed herself firmly against his hardness.

"Gabe, have you been with a woman before?" She stared at him, and he looked away, his face reddening.

She reached up and tilted his face back toward hers, running her fingers lightly over the scarred skin. "Have you?"

"No."

"Will you let me be your first?"

"I don't want your pity, Morgan," he said hoarsely.

She frowned. "It isn't pity, Gabe. I want you. I want you so much I can barely sleep at night."

She took his hand and rested it against her breast. He could feel her nipple pressing against his palm, and his hand squeezed reflexively. She inhaled and pressed her hips against him again.

"This has nothing to do with pity and everything to do with needing, wanting, to have you inside of me." She ran her fingers over his mouth, smiling a little when he thrust his pelvis against hers. "Will you take me to your bed, Gabriel?"

"Yes," he rasped.

"Good."

She pushed away from him and turned off the kettle before reaching for his hand. She linked their fingers together and led him down the hallway to his office. He frowned and followed her into the room.

"Morgan? What are you doing?"

"Do you have any condoms?"

"Shit. No." He gave her a look of dismay.

"May I use your laptop for a moment?"

He nodded and watched as she went online. She clicked the mouse a few times, and her fingers typed quickly over the keys before she held out her hand. "Come look at this."

He stared at the screen, realizing after a moment that he was looking at her medical records online.

"It's the results of the tests I had done a few years ago," she said. "I haven't been with anyone in three years, and I'm on the pill. If you're still not comfortable with that, I'll run into town and buy a box of condoms."

He shook his head. "No. I trust you, Morgan."

"Okay." She logged out and, holding his hand, led him to his bedroom. She reached for the light, and he covered her hand with his before she could flip the switch.

"Can we leave the lights off?" he asked.

"Yes." She smiled at him and tilted her face toward his. "Kiss me, Gabe."

He dipped his head and kissed her with a light, gentle brush of his mouth. She smiled and cupped the back of his neck, pulling him forward and pressing her lips against his. She traced his lips with her tongue, and when he opened his mouth, she slid her tongue in and lapped at his.

He groaned, and his hands shot out to grab her around the waist. He yanked her against him and kissed her hungrily. Already, he was bolder and more confident about kissing her, and when he flicked his tongue against her upper lip, she shuddered with need.

He slid his hands down and cupped her ass, squeezing it through her jeans. He pushed her against his cock as he kissed his way to her ear. He panted harshly in her ear as his big hands kneaded and squeezed roughly. He moved one hand to her breast and pulled at her nipple through her shirt and bra. She gasped, and he dropped his hand, staring at her anxiously.

"I'm sorry. Did that hurt?"

She shook her head. "No, that definitely didn't hurt."

She stepped back and stripped off her shirt before unbuttoning her jeans and pushing them down her legs. She stood in front of him in her bra and panties, and his face flushed with heat.

She tugged his shirt over his head and reached for the buttons on his jeans. He was wearing a pair of boxer briefs under them, and she traced the waistband with her finger. He shuddered all over and groaned loudly.

"Morgan, I don't know if I…"

He didn't want to tell her he was afraid he would come the minute she touched him.

She smiled and kissed him briefly. "I know. Just relax - we'll go slowly."

"I'm not sure that I can."

She smiled again and kissed his bare chest. "No matter what happens, it'll be amazing."

"I don't know about that," he muttered as she trailed a soft path of light kisses across his chest. Her mouth found his flat nipple, and when she sucked on it, he made a low groan.

"Oh my God, don't – don't do that, Morgan," he moaned.

"You don't like it?" she whispered before circling it with her tongue.

He arched his back. "No, I like it, I just -"

His cock was so hard it was painful, and he wasn't aware that he was pumping his lower body against hers until she pressed her hands against his hips. "Stop, Gabe."

"Please," he said.

She started to reach for his underwear, and he stepped back from her. "It's probably better if you don't touch me right now."

She nodded. "Take off your underwear."

He pushed them down his legs and stepped out of them, fumbling nervously as they tangled around his ankles. When he looked up again, she stood naked in front of him, and his ability to breathe was lost. He looked her up and down, his eyes lingering on her pink nipples and the dark curls between her thighs.

"You're so beautiful," he said, and she flushed prettily.

"You're beautiful too." She crawled onto his bed and lay on her back, patting the spot beside her. "Lie down, Gabe."

He didn't have to be told twice. He climbed onto the bed and relaxed on his side next to her. He couldn't stop staring at her breasts. He wanted to touch them again. He wanted to kiss them and taste her nipples.

As if she had read his mind, her soft hand cupped the back of his head and tugged his mouth toward her breast. He dipped his head and took one hard nipple into his mouth. She moaned at his touch and arched her back as he sucked lightly on the taut peak.

"Harder," she whispered, and he tightened his mouth around her nipple and pulled.

She shivered against him, her hands holding his head against her breast as he licked and tugged on first one nipple and then the next. He licked between her breasts and then cupped them with both hands, pushing them together so he could run his tongue from one nipple to the next. She twisted and moaned beneath him as he traced his tongue up to her collarbone and nipped lightly at it.

"Oh, Gabe," she whispered.

His cock throbbed and pulsed, and he realized that it was leaking all over her leg. Embarrassed, he pulled his pelvis away, and she frowned at him.

"What's wrong?"

"Nothing." He wanted to wipe the moisture from her leg before she saw it.

She followed his gaze, and his face heated up. "I'm sorry."

She shook her head. "There's nothing to be sorry about. I'm just as turned on as you are."

He gave her a doubtful look, and she took his hand and parted her thighs. "It's true, Gabe. Touch me, and you'll see."

She put his hand between her thighs and spread her legs further apart. "Touch me, honey."

His hand shaking, he pushed two fingers against her. She was warm and wet, and his fingers glided against her skin. Panting, he probed gently at her tight opening, groaning when his finger slid easily inside of her.

Her hips arched, taking more of his finger into her, and she moaned. He pulled his finger free, but when he tried to move his hand away, she clamped her thighs around it.

"No, don't stop, honey. It feels so good." She kissed him hard on the mouth, thrusting her tongue past his lips. She sucked on his lower lip and traced gentle fingers over his face. He didn't flinch when she stroked the scarred side of his face and then his chest. She ran her fingers across the bumpy skin as he pushed his finger back inside of her. He slid it in and out, watching her face as her eyes closed and she bit her bottom lip.

He licked her lip, and she opened her mouth so he could slide his tongue inside. She sucked hard on it, and he rubbed his cock against her smooth thigh. It was almost enough to make him come, and he forced himself to stop.

She reached down and took his hand. "Touch me here, Gabe."

She moved his fingers up to her clit and, holding her hand over his, moved his fingers in a circular motion. After a moment, she let go, and he continued to rub tentatively at the small pink nub. It was wet and slippery, and it swelled and hardened under his fingers.

"That's right, honey. Just like that. It feels so good." Her skin was flushed, and he watched as she began to pant and thrust her hips against his hand.

"Yes, oh yes," she moaned. Gabe rubbed harder, circling and pressing on her clit. Her fingers dug into his arm, and her whole body moved restlessly on the bed. He dipped his head and captured one nipple in his mouth. It was as hard as glass, and he sucked on it, rubbing her clit as she suddenly stiffened under him and her back arched up off the bed. She made a short cry of pleasure, and wetness filled his hand. She collapsed against the bed, panting harshly.

After a few minutes, she smiled at him. "Your turn."

She urged him on top of her, and he slipped between her legs, kneeling between them. She spread her legs wide, and he pushed his pelvis against hers, groaning in frustration and need when he slid against her wetness.

"Here – right here." She reached between them and took his cock in her hand, guiding it to her wet opening. He pushed and made a loud groan of pleasure when he sunk deep into her warm wetness.

"Oh God," he groaned.

He stayed perfectly still, his chest heaving for air, and she smiled up at him. "Your cock is so big, Gabe."

He stared down at her in surprise.

"What?" she asked.

"You – you never say bad words."

She grinned and tugged his ear down to her mouth. "Maybe it's because I've never had such a big cock in my pussy before."

"Christ, Morgan!" He cried out, his pelvis jerking against her as a pulse of pleasure went straight to his cock.

She sucked on his earlobe. "Does it feel good, Gabe?"

"Yes. You're so warm, Morgan."

"You're so thick, so hard." Her voice had deepened with desire, and he thrust hard into her in an involuntary response.

She made a cooing noise of pleasure and lifted her legs, planting her feet on the bed and squeezing his hips with her knees. "That's right, honey. Fuck me."

He shuddered all over, and then he was plunging in and out of her with hard, deep strokes. A small, dim part of him was afraid he was hurting her, but he couldn't stop. He closed his eyes, his breath rushing in and out of his lungs like a freight train as he thrust frantically within her.

She wrapped her legs around his hips and arched her body upward to meet each of his strokes.

"Morgan, oh God, Morgan…"

His balls were tightening, and every nerve in his body screamed in exquisite pleasure. She squeezed her pussy around his throbbing cock, and it threw him over the edge. He gave a hoarse shout and, his entire body spasming wildly, climaxed deep within her.

He jerked and twitched and shivered before collapsing weakly on top of her. She kept her legs wrapped around his hips and hugged him, kissing his shoulder as he panted above her. He rolled off her, and she curled up next to him, throwing one leg over his and snuggling up to him. She kissed his chest as he stroked her long hair.

"That was amazing."

She grinned and kissed his chest again. "Yes, yes, it was."

He looked down at her. "Was it – uh, did it…"

She nodded. "It was incredible, Gabe. I'm not saying that to stroke your ego. Also, you really do have the biggest cock I've ever seen."

He blushed furiously, and she laughed and kissed him hard. "I'm sorry. I didn't mean to embarrass you."

She turned on her side, and he curled up against her. He put his hand on her waist a bit timidly, and she grabbed it and put it on her breast. He cupped it tightly and buried his face in her neck as she yawned.

"Good night, Morgan."

"Night, Gabe."

CHAPTER 11

S he woke alone in the bed. The sun had been up for a while, and it was warm in the bedroom. She glanced at the alarm clock. It was after ten, and she stretched and slipped into one of his shirts before padding into the kitchen.

He stood in front of the sink, staring out the window with his back to her. She could tell immediately by the set of his shoulders that something was wrong.

She stood behind him and slipped her arms around his waist, placing a gentle kiss on his back through the fabric of his shirt. "Good morning, Gabe."

"Hi, Morgan."

She didn't say anything else, just continued to hug him and waited to hear what she already knew he was going to say.

* * *

GABE STARED MISERABLY OUT THE WINDOW. HE HAD WOKEN this morning at just after seven. It was already starting to warm up in the bedroom, and Morgan had kicked the sheets off in her sleep. He stared down at her body, marveling at how beautiful she was, at how every part of her was perfection.

He had leaned over her and placed a gentle kiss on her hip. He was starting to kiss up her ribcage when he caught sight of their reflections in the mirror across the room. His stomach dropped, and he sat up slowly. Next to her, his body looked even more grotesque. The morning light highlighted every scar on his body. He pushed away from her and sat on the side of the bed with his head in his hands.

She wanted him last night. He knew that. But she also nearly died last night. She was upset and worried about Vincent, and she reached out to him because she didn't want to be alone. She had said as much.

Don't be an idiot. It's more than that, and you know it.

He ran his fingers through his hair. Maybe it was, and maybe it wasn't. It didn't matter. Morgan deserved someone better. She was beautiful, and he was ugly. She was friendly, social, and outgoing and wouldn't be happy long-term being with someone who didn't like leaving his house. Even if he found the courage to go out publicly with her, the stares and whispers would eventually wear on her. There was no future for them, and he would be a giant asshole if he let her think there was just because he wanted to keep having sex with her.

Now, he pulled his shirt sleeves down and shifted against her, hoping she would take the hint and step back. She didn't. He could feel her breasts pressing against his back, and he cursed inwardly. His goddamn cock had a mind of its own, and he had to grip the sink tightly to stop from turning around and kissing her.

"Morgan, last night was incredible. It was the best night of my life," he said.

"But?" She rubbed his flat stomach, and his cock pressed painfully against the cupboards.

"But I don't think we should do it again."

"Why not?" She continued to rub his stomach, and he put his hands over hers, quelling their gentle movements.

"Because your friendship is really important to me. I don't want to lose it." He hoped like hell she wouldn't be pissed at him.

* * *

GABE WAS STIFF AS A BOARD, AND MORGAN COULD FEEL THE tension rolling off him. She knew he was lying, but she didn't press him. He was scared. He didn't believe she truly didn't see the scars on his body and was attracted to him because of who he was. His scarring on the outside was nothing compared to his emotional scars, and she knew if she pushed him too much, he would withdraw completely.

She sighed. Nothing she said would convince him. She would have to show him daily that she wanted and needed him. She would accept his terms and agree to be his friend, but she would also do everything in her power to seduce him and convince him they should be together.

Unfair.

Yeah, it probably was, but she decided she didn't care. She wanted Gabriel Dern and would do whatever it took to get him.

When he turned around, she pressed herself against his erection.

"Morgan, please -"

"It's fine, Gabe. We can just be friends," she said.

Relief crossed his face. "Thank you, Morgan. I'm sorry, I didn't mean -"

"We can return to being friends, but before we do, will you let me show you one more thing?"

He hesitated and then nodded. "Sure."

* * *

GABE DIDN'T KNOW WHAT MORGAN WANTED TO SHOW HIM, but her look of pure delight made him glad he agreed. He didn't object when she rose on her tiptoes and kissed him. He lifted his chin and groaned when she licked her way down his neck.

He wore his usual long-sleeved shirt and tensed when she slid her hands under the hem. Bright sunlight flooded through the windows, and even though she had already seen his upper body, he still wasn't comfortable with his shirt off in front of her.

He realized it wasn't his shirt she was reaching for but the waistband of his shorts. Quickly, before he could stop her, she pulled his shorts and briefs down and dropped to her knees. She stroked his cock with her soft hands, twisting lightly up and down the shaft as he groaned. He could feel her warm breath on his cock, and it took all of his willpower not to thrust it at her mouth.

"Morgan, what – what are you doing?"

"Showing you something," she whispered. She ran her thumb over the tip of his cock, sliding it through the drop of precum that had appeared before licking her thumb and smiling up at him.

"Oh my God," he moaned as she leaned forward and licked the head of his cock. His hands gripped the counter behind him, and he leaned against it for support as she licked him again. A groan tore from his throat, and he closed his eyes as she gripped the base of his shaft.

"Gabe." Her low voice broke through his haze of desire. "Open your eyes."

He opened his eyes and stared down at her as she smiled. "You'll want to watch this, honey."

He cried out when she slid her warm, wet mouth over his cock. She continued to grip the base of it, twisting lightly as she curved her tongue around the underside of his cock and sucked hard. She looked up at him, her eyes full of lust and need, and he couldn't stop himself from threading his fingers through her hair and gripping tightly as she bobbed her head back and forth over his cock.

She sucked on just the tip before circling it with her tongue as she stared up at him. He couldn't look away from her, couldn't stop watching the way her lips moved back and forth over his thick cock. She took more of him into her mouth, stroking him with her lips and tongue and hand, and dimly, he was aware of the loud moans of pleasure that were coming out of his mouth.

"Oh God, oh God, Morgan!" He was going to come. The feel of her warm mouth and the way her tongue stroked the underside of his cock had his legs trembling and his groin tightening.

She must have sensed it because she pulled him closer, one hand squeezing his ass and her other hand squeezing his cock, and wrapped her lips tightly around him. Her tongue flicked briefly against the head of his cock, and he shouted her name and arched his back. His hands tightened in her hair, and he watched as she swallowed his warm seed.

She released him with a soft, popping noise and climbed to her feet. She tugged his clothes up, kissed him lightly, and left the kitchen.

He heard her mutter as she tripped in the hallway and fell into the wall. He wanted to go to her, to make sure she was okay, but his legs were trembling, and he could barely stagger to one of the kitchen chairs. He collapsed on it, breathing harshly and wondering what the hell had just happened.

A few minutes later, she popped her head into the kitchen. She was dressed, and she gave him a cheerful smile. "What time are you picking up Vincent?"

"I – uh, what?"

"What time are you picking up Vincent?"

"Around one."

She frowned. "I told your sister I would go shopping with her this afternoon. I could cancel if you want me to go with you to pick him up."

He shook his head. "No, that's fine. I can pick him up."

"Okay. I'll pop by later this afternoon to see him. Is that okay with you?"

"That's – that's fine." The image of her on her knees in front of him, the sun shining in her hair, and her lips wrapped around his cock, wouldn't go away. He had a feeling it would be months before he stopped seeing it.

"Great. Bye, Gabe."

She was gone before he could tell her he wanted to return the favour.

* * *

SHE HAD TO HAND IT TO GABE. THE MAN HAD WILLPOWER.

She spent most of yesterday evening at his place. She cuddled and babied Vincent as Gabe made them dinner. The dog was doing surprisingly well after only a few days at home. His left front leg was swollen and tender to the touch but not broken like the vet had originally thought. The coyote had torn four long gashes in his stomach, but they were shallow, and the vet had sewn them together with neat black stitches.

She had worn tight jean cut-offs that were so short they barely covered the curve of her ass. She'd dusted off her rarely-used push-up bra and pulled a dark blue cami over it. She normally wore it under a t-shirt and hesitated for a few minutes about wearing just the cami. Ultimately, she decided to go for it, and after watching the way Gabe stared hungrily at her, she was glad she had.

She hadn't touched him once. She kept a careful distance between them and hoped he would make the first move. Her body was driving him crazy, she could see it every time he looked at her, and she stayed way later than she normally would.

She finally went home when she couldn't take it anymore. She had been about two minutes away from just throwing herself at him, and, with her body aching and throbbing for release, she gave him a hurried goodbye and nearly ran to her house.

Now, she sighed and continued to knead the bread dough. Okay, so it wasn't exactly going the way she hoped. It had been three days, and he hadn't cracked once, not even this afternoon when he was working in the backyard, and she decided it was the perfect time to sunbathe in her bikini.

It didn't mean she had to give up - she just had to rethink her strategy. She armed the sweat off her forehead, pushed her glasses up her nose, and wished that even a wisp of a breeze would come through the open kitchen window.

She continued to ponder her problem. Wearing very little clothing around Gabe wasn't working. Maybe she needed to up the ante and start touching him subtly. Or maybe she could arrange it so he accidentally walked in on her when she was showering.

She snorted and kneaded the dough furiously. She was being a fool. She had done her best, and Gabriel was obviously made of sterner stuff than she was. Or, he just wasn't as into her as she hoped. It wasn't the first time a guy hadn't been interested in her, but it bothered her more than any other time.

It was nearly two in the morning. She'd given up on sleep three hours ago and decided to make bread. It was a stupid decision, the house hadn't cooled down, and the oven was heating the kitchen to an almost unbearable level, but she didn't care.

Making fresh bread had been a weekly ritual with her mother, one that died with her. A few hours earlier, as she lay sleepless in her bed, she realized with a sudden sharp stab of pain just how much she had missed it. Measuring the ingredients, letting the dough rest, and then beginning the laborious work of kneading helped soothe her.

It wasn't just her horniness for Gabe that kept her awake. She had come very close to being mauled by coyotes in that field, and she suspected that she was not processing the trauma of that very well. At least the sleepless nights suggested she wasn't.

"What are you doing, Morgan?"

She screamed and clapped her hands against her chest. Flour flew up her nose, and she coughed and sneezed before glaring at Gabe through the screen of the kitchen window.

"Holy Hannah! You scared me so darn bad." She scowled at him.

"It's two in the morning. Why are you awake?"

"Why are you awake?" she countered.

"Vincent woke me. He needed to go to the bathroom. I saw your light when I took him out in the yard."

He disappeared from the window, and she heard him open the door and come in.

"You should keep the front door locked, Morgan. It's not safe for..."

His voice died off in a whispery little moan, and she glanced back at him. "What?"

He swallowed. "Nothing."

She eyed him suspiciously and then nodded to the kitchen chair. "Have a seat."

* * *

GABE WAS MORE THAN RELIEVED THAT MORGAN TURNED around and missed the way he collapsed bonelessly into the chair. He tried to keep his breathing slow and normal as he stared at her. She wore a barely-there sundress. The hem fell to just below her ass, and as she kneaded the ball of dough in front of her, the way her breasts jiggled clearly indicated she was braless. One of the thin spaghetti straps slipped down her arm, and she raked it back up with a mutter. It left a trail of flour on her tanned arm. For the first time since he had met her, she was wearing glasses, not contacts, and she looked ridiculously adorable in them.

"Why are you awake?" He ignored his raging hard on and wiped the sweat from his forehead. It was excruciatingly hot in the kitchen, and he licked his lips as he watched a bead of sweat drip down Morgan's throat to her chest and disappear inside her dress.

She shrugged. "Insomnia."

"So you decided to make bread? In the middle of the night?"

"Yes," she snapped irritably.

He stared in surprise at her. He had never seen her like this before and had no clue what to say or do.

* * *

125

MORGAN SLAPPED MORE FLOUR ONTO THE DOUGH AND continued to knead. It was pointless. She had already over-kneaded the darn thing, and she would have to chuck it in the garbage, but she had to do something to stop from throwing herself on Gabe and attacking him.

For once, he wasn't wearing a long-sleeved shirt. Instead, a thin white tank top clung to his flat stomach, and the shirt emphasized the muscles of his broad shoulders. She swallowed grimly and continued to pound at the dough.

She was hot and tired and horny and, if she was honest, a little embarrassed that she couldn't convince Gabe to have sex with her again. He had said it was the best night of his life, but he was also apparently finding it surprisingly easy to resist her.

Her face flushed. She'd never had any complaints before, and she knew that sometimes it was just a matter of compatibility, but she wasn't lying when she said it was amazing. For a virgin, Gabe had done a remarkably good job at making her come. Part of it was her deep attraction to him, and part of it was his bigger-than-average cock. She didn't think Gabe had any idea just how impressively big he was.

She slammed her hands into the dough so hard that the table shook. He was definitely blessed in that department, and while she'd always fallen firmly into the "size doesn't matter, it's how you use it" camp, she couldn't deny that it also felt unbelievably good when he fucked her.

He had come quickly like she knew he would. It was why she had gotten him to help her come beforehand. She knew he wouldn't last long, and she'd always taken longer than average to come from intercourse. She was shocked when, after only a few minutes of thrusting, an orgasm had rushed through her. She had squeezed around Gabe's cock compulsively, drawing his climax from him as the pleasure radiated through her body.

Christ.

She had to stop thinking about it. She had to stop thinking about Gabe sitting beside her and how easy it would be to –

Her hands clenched deeply into the dough when she felt his breath on her back. He had stood up and moved behind her silently. "What's this from?"

His fingers traced the large bruise on the back of her shoulder, and she shuddered all over, her fingers squeezing the dough. "I think it's from the night in the pasture when I fell holding Lemon."

He traced it again, and she jerked forward, banging her hip bones against the table. She winced as pain radiated down her legs.

His hands cupped her arms. "Are you okay?"

"Please stop touching me, Gabe," she muttered.

He stiffened and stepped away, sitting in the chair with a loud thump. Morgan turned and frowned at the hurt look on his face.

"Don't look at me like a hurt puppy," she groused. "You made up these rules, and I'm just trying to follow them."

"So I can't touch you ever?" He scowled.

She glared at him. "I repeat – your rules, not mine."

He folded his arms across his chest. "I didn't say anything about not touching. All I said was I thought it would be better if we were just friends."

"And I agreed to it. So we're just friends – isn't it great?"

"Yeah," he muttered and looked down at the floor.

"Yeah, for me, too."

She returned to the dough and grunted with frustration when he spoke again.

"I touched you before when we were friends. I don't see why it's changed."

"Well, it has."

"It shouldn't. Friends touch all the time. You taught me that."

Her temper snapped, and she whirled to face him. "Fine! You want to touch me? Go ahead and touch me!"

She stomped over and straddled him, dropping onto his lap and holding her dough-covered hands up in the air.

He swallowed hard, and a thread of satisfaction went through her when she felt his erection against her.

"Well? I'm waiting. You said you wanted to touch me, so do it."

He stared at her. "Morgan, what has gotten into you?"

She leaned forward until her breasts brushed against his chest, and her mouth was only inches from his. "What's gotten into me? You did, Gabriel. Four nights ago, you were between my legs, fucking me with that thick cock of yours. Or have you forgotten already?"

"No," he bit out, "I haven't forgotten."

"Then I guess fucking me wasn't that great for you. If it were, you'd understand why I don't want you touching me like friends do."

"I told you it was amazing - the best night of my life," he gritted through clenched teeth.

She put her mouth to his ear. "Then stop touching me, Gabe. Because every time you do, I can barely stop myself from tearing off your clothes and fucking you until you beg for mercy."

He groaned and then wrapped his hand in her ponytail and yanked her head back. He kissed her fiercely, and her lips parted under the intense assault. She returned his kiss, pouring all of her need and frustration from the last few days into one scorching kiss.

His hands gripped the front of her sundress and yanked. The thin straps didn't have a chance. They ripped with a low purring noise, and he jerked the thin material of her bodice to her waist, baring her breasts. He cupped them roughly, pulling on her nipples as she bent her head and bit the top of his shoulder.

He growled with pain and pulled back her head before dipping his head and latching onto the soft skin where her neck became her shoulder. She gasped in pain and pleasure at the feel of his teeth and reached for the waistband of his shorts.

She tugged at them desperately, and he raised his hips so she could rake them down his legs. He was naked under them, and she rubbed herself against his erection. He reached under her dress and curled his fingers into the crotch of her panties. He tore them from her body with an ease that surprised her and made her body throb with fresh lust.

She rose up, grabbed the base of his cock and impaled herself onto his thickness. She cried out with pleasure as he filled her, and she stretched around him.

"Gabe." She moaned low in her throat and grabbed the back of the chair, holding on tightly as his hard hands curved around her waist. He thrust in and out of her rapidly as he kissed and nipped her upper chest and shoulders.

She bounced up and down on his lap, pulling her glasses impatiently from her face when they slid down her nose and dropping them on the floor. She wrapped her arms around his broad shoulders and held on when he suddenly grabbed her ass and stood up, keeping his cock deep inside of her. He turned and set her on the table, pushing her flat on her back. She wrapped her legs around his waist, crossing her feet behind his back and pulling him deeper into her. He rested his hands on the table on either side of her head and fucked her so hard the table banged against the wall.

She panted and moaned as he slid in and out of her. Her head rocked back and forth on the hard table, and she came with a scream. Her body shook as he sank his cock deep into her pussy and came with a hoarse shout.

He laid on top of her, panting harshly in her ear as she stroked his back through his shirt. After a moment, he lifted his head and stared anxiously at her. "Did I hurt you?"

"No, not at all." She smiled at him. "You have dough in your hair now."

He grinned. "You're covered in flour."

She glanced down at herself. Her sweaty skin was dusty with flour, and she was pretty sure the sticky mess pressing into her back was the bread dough. He straightened and pulled her into a sitting position before peeling the lump of dough from her back.

"I think your bread is ruined."

She laughed. "Yeah."

He fingered the broken straps of her dress. "I ruined your dress."

"You can buy me a new one." She kissed him lightly on the mouth, pressing her bare breasts against him.

He hugged her hard and looked around as she buried her face in his neck. Flour and bits of dough were everywhere. "I'll help you clean up."

"Leave it. I'll clean it up later. Will you join me for a shower?"

He nodded and lifted her off the table. She shut off the oven and shimmied out of her ripped dress as he kicked off his shorts and picked up her glasses from the floor. She tugged at his shirt, and he hesitated briefly before allowing her to remove it. She kissed the scarred side of his chest gently and, leaving their clothes on the floor of kitchen, took his hand and led him to the bathroom.

CHAPTER 12

I t was bright in the bathroom. Gabe tried to ignore his feelings of vulnerability and exposure as Morgan turned on the shower. She wet her hand, adjusting the cold water until the water was cool, as he stared miserably at himself in the mirror above the sink. Every scar on his body stood out in stark relief, and he grimaced as she stepped into the tub and held out her hand.

"C'mon, Gabe."

He stepped into the tub with her and she closed the curtain around them. It blocked out some of the light, and he breathed a sigh of relief as she dipped her head under the spray of water, shuddering a little at the coolness as the water sprayed down over her body.

Her body was perfection – smooth skin and soft curves that made him ache to touch her. He reached out, caught a glimpse of the scarred skin on his left arm and dropped it back to his side. She blinked the water out of her eyes and stepped aside so he could take his turn under the water.

He turned so his right side faced her and started to inch

under the shower head. She scowled and took his arm, turning him to face her.

"Stop hiding from me, Gabe," she said. "You're beautiful. Everything about you is beautiful, and I hate it when you hide."

"Morgan, I -"

She pressed her wet fingers against his mouth. "No. Let me see you. Right now – right here. Close your eyes, honey."

She pushed him back gently under the spray of water, keeping his body facing hers, and he closed his eyes. He jerked a little at the first touch of her fingers on his scarred cheek. She touched him, exploring the valleys and bumps on his skin, and he couldn't keep his eyes shut. He needed to look at her. He needed to see the expression on her face as she examined him.

She was studying his face intently. She squinted adorably, and he supposed he was a bit fuzzy to her without her glasses or contacts. The thought soothed him a little. There was no disgust in her eyes and, more importantly, no pity. His hands moved without him realizing it, gripping her naked waist as he watched need and desire dance across her face.

She moved to his chest, stroking and touching his ruined flesh, examining every part of him without commenting. His cock was half-hard already as she lifted his left arm and ran her fingers down his biceps.

He gasped, and she stared up at him. "Does that hurt?"

"No."

She nodded and continued her gentle exploration. Her fingers skimmed down his side, and she raised an eyebrow at him when he squirmed.

"Tickles," he grunted, and she grinned at him.

"Good to know."

She made him turn around so she could examine his back. Her fingers traced along his body, and he groaned when she bent a little, and he felt her warm breath on his skin.

After what felt like an eternity, she straightened and pressed her wet, naked body against his back. He could feel her breasts, their nipples hard, pressing against him, and he clenched his hands into tight fists. God, he wanted her again already.

He wanted to be deep inside of her, wanted to hear her moaning his name, but he controlled himself fiercely. He didn't want her to think he was some sort of freak sex addict. He had no idea if being this horny so soon after sex was normal, and there really had been nothing sexual about her touching him.

She might find him attractive, burns and all, but pawing at her like some horny dog was bound to turn her off. He wished bitterly that he had some - hell *any* - idea of what was normal and how he was supposed to act.

She lathered soap between her hands and ran it over his wet skin. His cock, which had softened a bit as he worried internally, immediately stiffened again. He kept his back to her as she soaped his back and ass and legs. When her hands slid around to his front and gently washed the dough and flour from his chest, he gritted his teeth against the groan of need that wanted to escape. She lifted his arms and cleaned them thoroughly before her hands moved to his stomach.

His breath hissed between his teeth when she traced the hard muscles of his abdomen, the soap making her fingers move slickly across his skin. She kissed the left side of his neck, her lips pressing across the raised skin before she caught his earlobe in her mouth and worried it with her teeth.

"All clean," she whispered.

"Thanks." He cleared his throat.

"Well, almost all clean." She licked a drop of water from his scarred face. "I missed one spot, didn't I?"

"Yeah." He trembled violently when her hand slid from his abdomen to his dick, and she wrapped her long fingers around him.

"My God," she said when she realized how hard he was. "That was quick."

"I'm sorry," he muttered.

She kissed his neck again. "Sorry? Oh, honey, trust me – you have nothing to be sorry about. Do you have any idea how many men would kill to have this quick of a recovery time?"

Her hand stroked his hard shaft, and his hips moved with the motion of her touch. She peered around his arm to stare down at his cock, and he swelled in her hand at the look of dark lust on her face.

"So big," she muttered as she widened her fingers to keep a firm grasp on his throbbing, swelling cock. "So hard and so thick." Her voice had slowed and deepened into a low, honey-coated rasp, and he bucked against her in response.

"Touch yourself, Gabe," she said.

"I – what?" He blinked in surprise as she used her other hand to guide his right hand to his cock. She wrapped his fingers around it and then rubbed at his forearm.

"I want to watch you touching yourself." She smiled at him. "Show me how you make yourself feel good."

She kept her hand on his arm, small streams of water running down their bodies as he stroked his cock. She rubbed her breasts against his back and ran her hand over his stomach as he stroked back and forth. He moved slowly at first, feeling awkward and self-conscious, but her soft moans of approval and the way she continued to rub her naked body against his had his hand stroking harder and faster. He rubbed his thumb over the head of his cock, crying out with pleasure when she suddenly pinched his right nipple. His back arched, and he almost came in his hand.

"Do you have any idea how much I love fucking you, Gabe?" she asked as her hand came down and covered his. He moved his hand away, and she wrapped her fingers around his smooth shaft and mimicked the way he stroked it.

"The way your cock fills me up, how quickly you can make me come – that's never happened to me before." She made a small twisting motion with her hand, and he moaned loudly.

"I could spend hours riding your cock," she said. "Fucking you is all I think about anymore. You've turned me into a nymphomaniac."

She turned him around, her hand still gripping his shaft. She stroked harder, squeezing and releasing his cock in a rough rhythm that made his knees weak.

"Morgan, please," he rasped.

"Please, what?" She kissed him, and he thrust his tongue into her mouth with a desperation that embarrassed him.

"I need..." he moaned when she released his mouth.

"Need what?" she asked teasingly. "This?" She ran her fingers over the head of his cock. "Or maybe this?" She pumped him hard and fast, her fingers tightening around him as he cried out and thrust his pelvis against her.

"Tell me what you need, Gabe."

He wanted her mouth.

Oh God, how he wanted her mouth.

The last three days, when he wasn't thinking about burying his cock in her, he was remembering how she had looked on her knees in front of him. Remembering how hot and wet her mouth had been, the way her tongue had slicked across him, and how her lips had squeezed and tormented.

She was still stroking him, still driving him mad with her

135

soft hands, and he held her hips so tightly he could feel his fingers sinking into her soft flesh.

"Tell me." She bit his shoulder.

"Your mouth!" he cried out. "I need your mouth. Please, Morgan."

She immediately sank to her knees, opened her mouth wide and took half of his cock into her mouth with one smooth motion. She sucked hard, her cheeks hollowing out, and he cried out and tangled his fingers in her hair.

His hand tightened in the wet strands, and he thrust mindlessly into her mouth. Her hand reached between his legs and cupped his heavy balls gently for a few seconds before tracing the smooth patch of skin just behind them. She pressed, and he shouted with hoarse pleasure as his cock swelled and came hard into her mouth. She swallowed and licked and sucked until he was empty before rising to her feet.

He stared dazedly at her, and she gave him a delighted grin before pushing him gently away from the spray of water. He watched as she turned the hot water up and ducked under the water, quickly soaping and washing her entire body as he stood trembling behind her.

She peered at him as she rinsed the last of the soap from her smooth skin. "You okay, big guy?"

"Yeah, I – that was incredible," he said.

She grinned. "I'm glad you liked it."

He reached out and tugged her wet, naked body against his. "I'd, uh, I'd like to return the favour." He blushed a little.

She bit her lip, and her eyes darkened until they were almost the same shade of blue as his. "I'd like that too, Gabe."

She shut off the water, and they stepped out of the tub, toweling each other dry quickly. She took his hand to lead him to the bedroom and squealed with shock when he scooped her up. He carried her out of the bathroom and toward her bedroom.

He sat her on the bed, and she turned on the bedside lamp before wiggling back until there was space for him to kneel between her legs. He leaned down and placed a soft kiss between her breasts. She sighed with delight and kneaded at his shoulders.

He kissed the tender underside of each breast and then the sides, using his tongue to explore her soft, pale flesh until she was moaning quietly. Her nipples were rock hard, and he licked lightly along the tip of her right one.

"Gabriel." She said his name in a soft little moan, and he took her entire nipple into his mouth, sucking hard on it.

"Oh God. You are getting so good at this," she said.

"I was bad at it before?" he said teasingly.

She shook her head. "No - just a bit timid, maybe."

He bit down on her nipple, and she arched her back, a cry escaping her throat. He tugged on her nipple as she wrapped her legs around his thighs and rubbed her pelvis against him. He switched to her other breast, teasing it with his teeth and mouth until she whimpered with need.

"Too rough now?" He licked her nipple, and she shook her head again.

"No, Gabe. It feels so good."

He kissed his way down her body, tasting every part of her skin with his tongue. He stopped at the scar on her stomach, remembering the way he had wanted to kiss it the first time she showed it to him, and spent extra time kissing and licking the raised skin.

He kissed her hip bones and traced each rib with his tongue before he said, "Turn over, Morgan."

She rolled onto her stomach, and he straddled her hips and traced his fingers up and down her back. She giggled and twisted her head to look back at him. "That tickles."

He grinned at her. "Good to know."

He leaned over her and lightly kissed the bruise on her back.

"That night, when I heard you scream in the dark and the rain, I nearly went crazy," he confessed as he leaned over her and swept her hair to the side so he could kiss the back of her neck. "If I hadn't gotten home when I did…"

He kissed her soft cheek, and she turned her head to kiss his mouth. "You got there in time. I'm fine."

"Are you?" He stroked her cheek.

She nodded. "Yeah, I think so. I haven't been sleeping all that great the last few days, but I'm not sure if that's because I missed you or because of the near-death experience."

He kissed the tip of her nose. "I missed you too, honey."

She smiled at the endearment, and he blushed a little before kissing her smooth back again. She took a trembling breath and arched her back as he licked her spine. He scooted down until he was straddling her knees and stared appreciatively at her ass.

"You have a great ass," he said and then blushed again.

She laughed and wiggled it at him. "Thank you."

He stroked her ass, his fingers squeezing and pressing, and her laughter turned into a low moan. He rubbed the back of her thighs and then pulled on her hip, urging her to turn over. She did, and he knelt between her legs again and stared at the dark curls between her thighs.

She must have sensed he was nervous because she sat up and cupped his face. "If you don't want to do this, you don't have to."

He kissed her. "Trust me – I want to do this." The blush that still lingered in his cheeks deepened. "I'm a little worried I won't do it right."

She smiled. "Whatever you do will feel good. Honestly."

He gave her an anxious look, and she grinned at him. "If

you don't get it right this time, I'll make you practice twice a day until you do. Deal?"

He snorted laughter. "Deal."

"Good." She kissed him lightly on the lips and relaxed on the bed. She widened her thighs, smiling a little at the way his eyes darkened when her sex was exposed to him.

"You just gonna look at it, handsome? Or start practicing?" She arched her eyebrow at him.

He stretched out on his stomach and kissed the inside of her thigh. "Definitely start practicing."

He bent his head and kissed the soft curls between her legs. He slid his hands under her ass and lifted her slightly, tilting her hips up until his warm breath washed over her. He kissed her, his nervousness disappearing when she immediately moaned. He instinctively searched for her clit with his tongue. The pink nub was already hard and swollen, and he licked it delicately. Her hands knotted in his hair, and she arched her hips into his mouth as he moved one hand to her tight opening. He slid his finger into her as he licked her clit, and was rewarded with another loud and husky groan.

* * *

MORGAN SIGHED AND TWISTED HER FINGERS INTO GABE'S HAIR. His inexperience was an advantage as far as she was concerned. Nervous about hurting her, every movement he made with his tongue and fingers was soft and delicate, and it brought her quickly to the brink. His relentless, gentle touching was driving her need to a fevered pitch, and she twisted and moaned against him, her hips arching continuously against his mouth.

"Oh my God, Gabriel," she panted when he slid another finger into her warm core. He pushed them in and out and then sucked on her clit. She shouted his name, her hips bucking wildly and her entire body squirming as she came in a burst of sweet pleasure.

Vaguely she was aware of him sliding up her body, of his hard cock suddenly probing at her opening. She was completely drenched, and her body accepted his cock eagerly, stretching to accommodate his width as he plunged fully into her.

"Morgan," he rasped, and her eyelids fluttered open. She inhaled sharply at the raw intensity in his gaze, and her thighs tightened around his hips.

"You're so beautiful," he groaned as he moved within her in a thick slide and retreat motion.

"So are you," she said. "I love fucking you, Gabe. Do you love fucking me?"

"Yes," he moaned.

"Tell me," she demanded.

"I love fucking you, Morgan," he said against her lips, and she shuddered and tightened her core around him. Her warm and velvety pussy clung snugly to him, and he propped himself above her and thrust in and out with hard movements.

"Say it again," she murmured.

"I love fucking you, Morgan."

She kissed him hard, her tongue twisting and turning in his mouth as she slid her hands around him and clung to his back. Her fingers dug into his scarred skin, but he ignored the dull pain and drove deep into her. She cried out, her body shuddering under his as a second orgasm flooded through her. He groaned and plunged into her twice more before the squeezing of her pussy drove him over the edge, and he came hard inside her.

He pulled out and collapsed on his back on the bed beside her. She turned and snuggled up to him, throwing her leg over his waist and resting her head on his chest. He stroked her long hair as she ran her fingers over his scarred flesh.

Morgan sighed contently. Her entire body was limp and warm, and she was already starting to drift off when his voice rumbled above her. "So, what's the verdict?"

"Hmm?"

"Do I need to practice twice a day?" There was a hint of smugness in his voice, and she pinched him lightly.

"Maybe just once a day." She yawned and curled up closer to him. "Stay with me tonight?"

"Yes," he said and pulled her against him. "Good night, honey."

"Good night, handsome," she murmured.

CHAPTER 13

"Do you like pancakes?" Gabe paused with the pancake mix in his hand.

"I do," Morgan said

It was late the next morning, and they were at the farmhouse. She was sitting on one of the kitchen chairs and gently petting the top of Vincent's head as Gabe made them something to eat.

Gabe stirred the pancake batter while waiting for the pan to heat up. "Last night was amazing, Morgan. I want you to know that."

"But?" she said.

"No buts. It was amazing."

She grinned at him. "Yeah, it was."

He laughed as she tucked her feet up under her and continued to stroke Vincent's soft head.

"What do you have planned for the rest of today?" she asked.

"I need to do some work. How about you?"

She shrugged. "Not a whole lot. I need to pack."

He gave her a puzzled look as he poured batter into the pan. "Pack for what?"

"A friend of mine from the city is getting married this weekend. I'm returning for that and visiting with some of my friends. I haven't been back since I moved, and I miss them." She smiled at him.

"When do you leave? How long will you be gone?" He could feel panic rising in him, and he tamped it down. It was ridiculous to be upset that Morgan was leaving.

"I leave tomorrow and -"

"Tomorrow? You're leaving tomorrow? Why didn't you tell me?"

"I'm only gone for a week. I'll be back next Saturday. I didn't tell you because I was too busy trying to seduce you instead of talking to you."

She winked at him, and he gave her a weak smile before returning to the pancakes. The batter was bubbling like crazy, and he flipped it before it could burn. His stomach clenched painfully at the thought of Morgan being gone for a week.

He jumped when her soft hands slipped around his waist, and she leaned against his broad back. "It's only a week, Gabe."

"Yeah." He cleared his throat. "Where will you stay?"

"With friends. I'll probably couch surf at a few different places. My friend Alex said I could stay with him for as long as I needed."

He stiffened. "Alex is a guy?"

She squeezed his waist and kissed his back through his t-shirt. "Alex is sixty-two years old and has a boyfriend."

She laughed when he visibly relaxed, and she tugged on his t-shirt until he turned around. Her eyes were dancing with laughter, and he blushed. "Sorry."

"Don't be." She kissed his chin and smiled at him. "You

know - you could come with me. You could be my date for the wedding, and I could show you the city and introduce you to my friends."

He stiffened again and pulled away from her, turning around to take the pancake out of the pan before pouring more batter into the hot pan. "That's not a good idea, Morgan."

She rubbed his back. "I think it is."

"Well, it isn't. I can't go with you. I have the farm to look after, and I can't just leave at the drop of a hat."

"Peter and Lacey would look after the farm if you asked," she said.

"Drop it, okay? I can't go with you," he retorted as he flipped the pancake.

"Okay."

He turned back to face her, steeling himself against the hurt on her face. "We should keep what's happening just between the two of us. People like to talk in this town, and I don't think it's a -"

She backed away from him and crossed her arms over her torso. "Do you want to go back to just being friends, Gabe? Is that what this is? Because if it is, then just say it."

"No." He moved toward her and pulled her against him. "I don't want to be just friends. I can't be just friends with you, Morgan."

"Then why the big secret?" She frowned at him.

He sighed harshly. "You don't know what it's like in this town. It's a small place, and people like to talk. I don't want people thinking less of you because you're dating the town freak."

She kicked him in the shin hard enough to make him wince, and he scowled at her. "What was that for?"

"Don't you ever call yourself a freak again, Gabriel Dern. Do you hear me? The next time you do, it won't be your shin

145

I kick!" She gave him her own scowl as she backed away from him.

"I'm trying to protect you."

"I don't need to be protected. I'm a big girl, and I can take care of myself. Besides, I don't care what the people in this town say or think about me."

"I do. I want to be with you, but I'd feel better if people didn't know right now. I don't want them judging you. Is that so awful of me?"

He gave her a pleading look, and she sighed and looked down at the floor. "No, it isn't. But I won't hide from people forever, Gabe. Do you understand?"

"I do." He nodded. "I just – I just need some time." He started to reach for her and hesitated. He wasn't sure if he should touch her or not, and relief rushed through him when she stepped toward him and buried her face in his chest.

He put his arms around her and hugged her fiercely. "Thank you, Morgan."

"You're welcome." His shirt muffled her voice. "Your pancakes are burning."

"Shit!" He let her go and pulled the black and smoking pancake out of the pan as she retreated to her chair.

* * *

GABE SHIFTED IN THE LAWN CHAIR AND WONDERED IF HE HAD been here long enough to say his goodbyes. Probably not. They had just finished supper, and Peter was planning a bonfire.

He sighed and ignored the broad smile that Sally gave him from across the yard. He shouldn't have come tonight, but it was Peter's birthday. Now that he regularly appeared for their barbecues, Lacey threatened to disown him if he hadn't come to the party.

Plus, he was lonely and bored without Morgan. She returned tomorrow, and he couldn't wait to see her again. She had texted him daily, and they had spoken on the phone every night, but it wasn't the same as being with her.

He saw Sally making her way toward him, and he stood and walked quickly into the house, hoping to escape her not-so-subtle advances.

* * *

"Happy Birthday, Peter."

Peter turned and grinned delightedly at Morgan.

"Morgan! What are you doing here?" He hugged her hard.

"I decided to come back a day early. Lacey told me it was your birthday, so I thought I'd pop by and join the party before heading home."

"I'm so glad you did. And I know that Lacey will be thrilled."

"Morgan!" Lacey hurried over and hugged Morgan. "You're back!"

"I couldn't miss Peter's birthday bash," Morgan said.

"I am pretty awesome," Peter said.

Lacey laughed and slapped him on the butt. "Yeah, yeah, Mr. Awesome. Get over there and start your bonfire."

"Yes, ma'am." Peter tipped an imaginary hat and walked toward the fire pit as Lacey turned back to Morgan.

"So, how was your trip? Did you have a good time?"

"I did. The wedding was beautiful, and it was nice to see my friends again." She smiled a little. "Although I missed this place like crazy."

Morgan was mostly telling the truth. She'd missed the little town she now called home and wanted to be home in time for Peter's birthday, but it was Gabe that she had really

147

come home early for. She missed him so much that it felt like a physical ache.

She glanced casually around. Gabe had told her he was going to the party but was nowhere to be seen.

"Did you go home first?" Lacey asked.

Morgan shook her head. "No, I took an Uber from the airport to here." She pointed to her suitcase, which was tucked neatly against the side of the house. "I figured I could hitch a ride home with your brother."

When Lacey didn't reply, she cleared her throat and glanced around again, her cheeks reddening. "Did Gabe come to the party tonight?"

"Yes. He's…" Lacey trailed off and gave Morgan a small, considering look.

Morgan's blush deepened, and Lacey's eyes suddenly widened.

"Oh my God," she said. "You and my brother are a couple, aren't you?"

"Lacey…" Morgan didn't want to lie to her, but she'd promised Gabe to keep their relationship a secret.

"Holy shit, you are!" Lacey squealed and hugged her hard. "I can't believe I didn't see it. Oh my God, this is amazing."

"Lacey, be quiet," Morgan said in a low voice.

"What? Why?"

"Because your brother and I haven't told anyone, and he's asked me to keep it quiet."

"Keep it quiet? Why on earth for?"

Morgan sighed. "It's a long story, and I'll tell you later, okay? Just for now – can you keep it to yourself?"

Lacey nodded, and Morgan smiled at her. "Thank you."

"Don't mention it. Gabe went into the house a few minutes ago. I imagine he'll be thrilled to see you." Lacey squeezed her arm and snickered. "Why don't you say hello?"

"I think I will," Morgan said primly and walked toward the house, Lacey's soft giggling echoing in her ears.

* * *

GABE LEFT THE BATHROOM AND STARTED DOWN THE HALL toward the patio doors. He would say goodbye to Peter, Lacey, and Natalia and head home. He was miserable being here without Morgan, and if he had to listen to Sally prattle on for another minute, he'd –

"Hi, Gabe."

He looked up, groaning inwardly as he pasted on a neutral smile. "Hi, Sally."

The small blonde stood in the living room doorway, blocking his path to the patio doors at the far end of the room.

"You've been avoiding me tonight."

"No, I haven't."

She smiled a little and took a few steps forward until she stood before him. "Have I done something to upset you?"

He shook his head. "No, of course not."

"Then why won't you let me touch you?"

"I don't like to be touched, Sally."

"Maybe you just haven't had the right person touch you." She smiled at him, her eyes skittering over the left side of his face, and he felt the slow burn of anger at the look of pity in her eyes.

"That isn't it. It's -"

He made a muffled sound of surprise when Sally launched herself at him and mashed her mouth down on his. Completely shocked, he stood there as she wrapped her arms around his waist and pressed her body against his. The feel of her tongue pushing at his lips broke his stunned stillness.

149

He pushed her away, and she drew her full lips into a pout. "Gabe, you -"

"Am I interrupting something?"

Sally spun around and frowned at Morgan as Gabe's heart skipped a fucking beat. "Actually, you are."

"I'll give you your privacy." Morgan gave her a brittle smile, slid by them, and walked down the hallway to the bathroom.

Sally reached for Gabe's hand, and he yanked it out of her grip. "Stop it. I'm not interested in you. Do you understand that?"

She flushed, and her soft and pretty features turned ugly. "Frankly, you should be happy that someone like me is interested in you. I can't imagine you have many women knocking down your door to date you."

He ignored the flush of embarrassment rushing through him and gave her a look of such cold hatred that she withered a little under it. "Get lost, Sally. You're pathetic."

She snorted angrily and stomped away as he turned and hurried to the bathroom. He knocked lightly on the door. "Morgan? Let me in. I can explain."

"It's not locked," she said.

He turned the handle gingerly and stepped into the small room. He closed the door behind him and stared at her. She stood next to the tub, and he couldn't tell what she was thinking from the expression on her face.

"Morgan – what you just saw wasn't what it looked like. I swear. I had no idea she would kiss me."

She remained silent and panic gnawing at his belly, the words spilled out of his mouth. "I was avoiding her all night. I was coming out of the bathroom, and she trapped me in the hallway. You have to believe me. I'm not interested in her. If I had known that she was going to do that, I wouldn't have -"

"Gabe – stop," she said.

He trailed to a stop and gave her a miserable look as she stepped toward him. "I believe you."

"You do?"

She nodded. "Of course I do. I saw her throw herself at you, and I saw you push her away. Besides, you're not the kind of guy who screws around on a woman."

"I – thank you?" he said.

She laughed. "You're welcome."

He stared at her, feeling awkward and unsure, and she gave him a small grin. "Are you going to stand there, or are you going to kiss me?"

He reached for her, his heart thumping loudly in his chest, and she crossed the small distance between them and tucked her body against his. He cupped the back of her head and kissed her. She wrapped her arms around him and returned his kiss. Their tongues teased softly at first and then with more urgency as he reached down and slipped his hand under her dress. He gripped her firm thigh and pulled her leg up around his waist before grinding his pelvis against hers.

"I missed you."

"I can tell," she said breathlessly.

"Did you miss me?" He kissed her neck as she took his hand and guided it between her legs. Her panties were soaked, and pure and primal need went through him.

"The entire flight home, I kept imagining all the things I would do to you when I finally saw you again," she said. "I kept thinking about how good it would feel to have you between my legs."

"Let's get out of here," he groaned into her ear.

She shook her head. "We can't. I just got here, and there's still the bonfire."

"I don't care. I need you right now." He slipped his fingers under the edge of her panties and rubbed her wet clit. "And you need me. I can tell."

She moaned, and then she pushed him back and wiggled out of her panties.

"Morgan? What -"

"Shh." She turned around and leaned against the small cabinet that housed the sink. "Take me right now, Gabe."

"What? Morgan – we're at my brother-in-law's birthday party. We can't just…"

His voice died as she shimmied her skirt up around her waist. He stared at her bare ass, his cock suddenly rock-hard in his jeans, as she smiled at him.

"We can have sex right now, or you can wait a few hours. Take your pick, Gabe."

He reached for his belt, unbuckling it hurriedly before unbuttoning his jeans. He tugged his cock free, and Morgan made a soft sound of pleasure and reached behind her. She held his cock in one hand, stroking it with her thumb as he pushed up against her.

"I've missed your cock," she moaned as he rubbed his throbbing cock between her ass cheeks. "Quickly, Gabe. I can't wait."

She bent over the sink and spread her legs. He could see her opening glistening wetly, and with a soft groan, he guided his cock into her. He shoved himself in to the hilt, his pelvis slapping up against her bare ass.

She gasped sharply as he pumped in and out of her, bracing herself against the sink as he reached around and cupped her breasts through her shirt and bra. He could barely feel her nipples, and with a grunt of frustration, he shoved his hands under her shirt and pushed her bra up, freeing her breasts.

He cupped them roughly. Her nipples were hard against his palms, and he groaned when Morgan thrust her hips backward, taking him even deeper into her wet warmth.

"Shh, Gabriel." She slapped him lightly on his hand. "Do

you want the others to know you're fucking me in the bathroom?"

He shuddered and plunged back and forth, gripping her hips as she met him stroke for stroke. She rubbed her clit in tiny circles, her breath coming in harsh pants as he thrust in and out of her.

She suddenly stiffened against him, her hand clamping down on the sink as she climaxed around his dick. She buried her face into her arm, muffling her cry of pleasure as Gabe pushed in and out of her tight core. Moments later, he muffled his cry as he thrust once more into her and came. She straightened, and he hugged her, burying his face in the back of her neck as she squeezed his arms.

He eased out of her, and she turned and kissed him on the mouth as he tucked his cock back into his jeans and buttoned them. She fixed her bra and shirt and straightened her skirt before smiling at him. "Go back to the party. I'll be out in a minute, okay?"

He nodded and kissed her again. "I'm glad you're back, honey."

"Me too." She rubbed the tip of her nose against his and smacked him lightly on the ass. "Go on, handsome. I'll be right out."

CHAPTER 14

Gabe stood up and stretched. The fire had died down to embers, and the party guests were starting to leave. He and Morgan had been here long enough. He would find her, they would say their goodbyes, and he would take her home to his bed.

His dick stirred in his pants at the thought. The quickie in the bathroom had only flamed his lust for her. He was tired of pretending to be interested in the useless chatter of Peter's friends. He had sat across from Morgan at the bonfire, the flames flickering between them, and every glance from her had brought a new surge of desire to his body.

He headed toward the house. Morgan had disappeared into the house with Lacey nearly fifteen minutes ago. He stepped through the patio doors and scanned the living room. It was empty, and he frowned and headed toward the door to the hall. She must be in the kitchen.

"So, are you going home with our resident freak tonight or what, Sally?"

Gabe froze as Sally's voice drifted in from the hallway.

"Why? You jealous, Derek?"

Gabe stepped closer to the doorway, a mixture of embarrassment and anger churning in his belly.

"Jealous of what?" the man scoffed. "His hideous-looking face? Or his high-end career as a sheep farmer?"

There was a smattering of laughter as Gabe's hands curled into fists. There were at least two other women in the hallway with Sally and Derek, and he took a deep breath and told himself to turn around and walk back outside. What they were saying wasn't anything he hadn't heard before.

A woman's voice, soft and hesitant, said, "Sally, what on earth are you thinking? Gabe Dern is a recluse. He never leaves his house, and my friend Karen says he's quite nasty."

"You'd think with a face like his, he'd work harder on his personality." Another woman's voice chimed in. "Am I the only one who thinks Lacey and Peter's parties have become a real drag since he started showing up? I can hardly look at his face, and he sits there like a lump, staring at you with his creepy blue eyes."

Sally gave a spiteful little laugh. "If you think the scars on his face are bad, you should see the ones on his chest. It's like a cheese grater attacked him."

"And how would you know, Miss Sally?" Derek said lazily. "Did you end up throwing the sheep farmer some pity sex when you were so sweetly taking care of him?"

"No! I showed up early one night and caught him changing. It was awful. His chest and back are a horrid mess of scars. You'd have to see it to believe it."

"Why did you offer to help him out, Sally?" The second woman's voice asked. "You weren't actually attracted to him, were you?"

"No. I just felt sorry for him. Lacey's my friend, and I figured he could use some company. Lacey said he spends all his time out there alone, and she was worried about him. I only managed a couple of weeks before I had to stop going over there. Honestly, he has the personality of a rock."

She hesitated and said, "He made a couple of passes at me. I'm probably the first woman who's shown interest in him in years. I turned him down politely, but he was getting pretty desperate."

Derek laughed. "Why would he be desperate when he has all those sheep just waiting for him in the barn? They don't care what he looks like."

"Eww, gross! Derek, that's disgusting." Sally laughed despite her statement, and the other two women giggled with her.

Gabe turned to leave, his face bright red and his stomach churning.

"What?" Derek said innocently. "If you think he isn't having sex with those sheep of his then -"

"Shut your fucking mouth, you ignorant asshole."

Gabe's eyes widened, and he groaned in dismay at the sound of Morgan's voice. He ran toward the doorway as Morgan spoke again.

"Say one more word about Gabriel, and I'll punch you in the goddamn face. Do you hear me?"

Gabe skidded to a stop. Morgan stood in the hallway. Her face was red with anger, and her entire body shook. She glared one-by-one at the group of people in the hallway, her gaze landing on Sally last, and the woman shrank under the fury of Morgan's gaze.

"Gabriel Dern is a better person than any of you idiotic mouth-breathers will ever be," Morgan snapped. "Maybe you should try telling the truth, Sally. Or are you too embarrassed to admit that you hit on Gabe, and he turned you down flat."

The others glanced at Sally, and Morgan nodded. "That's right. Your shallow little friend here thought he'd be an easy lay because of the way he looks. Only it didn't work out so well for you, did it, Sally? Remind me how many times you hit on him only to have him say no. Was it four or five times?"

"Shut up, Morgan," Sally said.

"Why don't you make me shut up?" Morgan said.

Gabe blinked at the unexpected venom in her voice. She bore no resemblance to the soft-spoken school teacher she normally was, and he stepped quickly into the hallway. "Morgan, it's time to go."

The others turned to stare at him. Morgan glanced at him, and her fury seemed to grow. "I'm not finished yet."

"Uh, yeah, I think you are. Come on, I'll give you a ride home."

She stared at him and then reached out and took his hand. "Fine, take me home."

He started to lead her away, but she tugged on his hand. As he turned to look at her, she crushed her body against his and kissed him hard on the mouth. He stepped back, his hands automatically going around her waist as she kissed him.

She released his mouth and stared at Sally. "He turned you down because he thinks you're awful and boring."

Sally started to speak, and Morgan stared her down before saying, "I don't think you're awful or boring. I just think you're the stupidest fucking person ever to walk the planet. Gabe's with me, and even if he weren't, he'd never be interested in someone like you."

As she started leading Gabe into the living room, Derek said, "It's a small step up from the sheep, I guess."

Gabe stiffened in anger. With a loud curse, he turned and shoved Derek up against the wall. A picture fell, and the glass shattered.

Lacey stepped into the hallway. "What the hell is going on?"

Gabe pinned his arm across Derek's throat and placed his ruined face only inches from the smaller man's. "Say one more word about her, and I'll send you to the hospital. Do you understand?"

Derek stared wide-eyed at the scars on Gabe's face and didn't answer.

"Do you understand?" Gabe shouted and shook him roughly.

"Yes! I understand!" Derek cringed against the wall when Gabe let him go.

Gabe brushed past the others and took Morgan's hand. He led her toward the patio doors as Derek rubbed his neck with his hand.

"You're a goddamn freak!" he shouted as Gabe opened the door, and he and Morgan disappeared into the darkness.

* * *

"Gabe." Morgan followed Gabe into the farmhouse's kitchen, petting Vincent and Delilah absentmindedly.

He stared out the window, his hands resting on the sink as she approached him gingerly.

"Don't shut me out, Gabe."

He sighed. "I'm not."

"You are. We need to talk about what happened at the party."

He turned to face her, and her heart ached at the embarrassment on his face. "What's there to talk about? I knew something like this would happen, and it did."

"It doesn't matter. I don't care what those idiots think or say."

"You shouldn't have defended me."

She stared at him in confusion. "Gabriel, I will always defend you."

"This is exactly why I knew this wouldn't work."

"What are you talking about? Since when is it a bad thing to defend the person you lo-"

She stopped and pressed her lips together. "Tell me why defending a person you care about is bad."

He folded his arms across his chest. "Morgan, what happened tonight is just a taste of what you'd have to deal with regularly. I'm the town fre-"

"Don't you dare say it," she warned him.

"We both know what I am, and there will always be people like Sally and Derek to remind us of it."

"So what? You shouldn't care what those assholes think or say. I don't. I only care about how I feel about you and how much I want to be with you."

"This isn't going to work, Morgan."

Panic went through her, and she rushed forward. She put her arms around his waist, but he kept his crossed firmly across his chest and stared at the floor. She took his chin and lifted it until he was looking at her.

"Don't say that, please. You're so important to me, and I can't -"

"Morgan, stop. It isn't fair for me to drag you into my fucked-up life. I was wrong to start a relationship with you, and I'm sorry. I refuse to let you spend your life defending me and being forced to go places alone because I won't go with you."

"Gabe -"

"We're too different. You're outgoing and social, and I'm – well, I'm me. I don't like to go out and be with people, and you might be fine with that now, but eventually…"

She shook her head. "You're wrong, Gabe. I am perfectly content staying at the farmhouse with you, and if I want to go out and you don't – I'll go out. I don't need you holding my hand every moment of the day. You know that."

She cupped his face and rubbed his scarred cheek. "You're scared. I get that. I do. But don't let that fear be your excuse for living alone for the rest of your life."

He tore away from her. "What do you want from me?"

"I want you to believe you're good enough for me just the way you are," she said.

"I'm not!" he roared. "Listen to me, for God's sake! I'm not good enough for you and never will be."

"Yes, you are! Gabe, you're -"

"I want you to leave, Morgan. This was a huge mistake, and I should never have allowed you to get this close to me."

"Fine. I'll go. Get some rest, and tomorrow we'll talk more, okay?"

He shook his head. "No. It's not a good idea. I – we can't be together anymore. Not as lovers or as friends."

Her lips started to tremble, and she swallowed audibly. "You don't mean that."

"I do. I was using you, Morgan. I wanted to have sex, and you were willing."

She stared up at him. She knew he'd only said it to drive her away, but it was like he'd stabbed her in the damn heart.

"Liar," she said before stalking out of the kitchen.

CHAPTER 15

"Hi, Uncle Gabe!"

"Hi, Nat." Gabe smiled at the young girl as she hopped out of the car. He picked her up and kissed her soft cheek.

"How was trick or treating last night?"

"Good. I got lots of candy."

"Well, make sure you don't eat it all at once. You'll get a tummy ache."

The little girl rolled her eyes. "I know. Daddy already told me that. I had to eat all my supper tonight before I could even have one piece of candy."

Gabe smiled and set her down on the ground. Vincent and Delilah crowded around her, and she giggled as they licked eagerly at her hands and face.

"Hi, Peter."

"Hello, Gabe. How are you?"

"Can't complain. Where's Lacey?"

"She's, uh, visiting a friend." Peter looked away, and Gabe sighed.

The friend would be Morgan. A week after he told her he

couldn't be with her, she moved out of the guesthouse. It had been over two months, and he had no idea how she was or where she was living. Lacey refused to tell him. His sister was angry and disappointed with him when he wouldn't tell her why he had driven Morgan away.

"I know you two were dating, Gabriel," she said about two weeks after Morgan moved out. "I guessed it the night of Peter's birthday party. Why did you break up with her?"

"Didn't Morgan tell you?"

"She won't talk about it. I know it had something to do with that silly little bitch Sally and whatever the hell happened in the hallway that night. All Morgan would say is that you broke up with her."

"How is she?"

Lacey glared at him. "If you want to know, then ask her yourself, you giant idiot. You've made a mistake, Gabriel. Morgan was the best thing that ever happened to you, and you know it."

He sighed and stared into his cup of coffee. "Please, Lacey. I don't want to talk about it, okay?"

Her gaze softened at the look of pain on his face, and she reached out and took his hand. "It's not too late, Gabe. You can still fix this. Morgan cares for you deeply."

"It is too late. Can we just drop it?" He had nearly pleaded, and she had finally relented, changing the topic to other things.

Now, he cleared his throat and crouched beside Natalia. "How is school going, honey?"

"Fine. I miss Ms. Wilson. I don't like the new teacher." The little girl pouted briefly.

"Well, you're in grade two now. You knew you'd have a different teacher this year." Gabe patted her gently on the back.

"Nu-uh, Uncle Gabe. Ms. Wilson got moved to be the grade two teacher. She's my teacher again this year."

He frowned at her in confusion as Peter cleared his throat. "Nat, why don't we visit Lemon?"

"Okay!" Nat took Gabe's hand. "C'mon, Uncle Gabe. Take me to see Lemon."

"Just a minute, Nat." He glanced at Peter. The man looked decidedly uncomfortable, and Gabe started to get a bad feeling in his stomach.

"Honey, if Ms. Wilson teaches grade two, why do you have a new teacher?" Gabe asked.

"Because Ms. Wilson is sick. She's in the hospital," Natalia said. "Can we go see Lemon now?"

The blood draining from his face, Gabe stood up and stared at Peter. "What's wrong with her? Why is she in the hospital?"

Peter cursed under his breath. "Gabe, she's fine. She just – she cut herself, and it got infected. She didn't go to the doctor, and it turned into a pretty bad blood infection."

"How bad?"

"Pretty bad. She went into the hospital four days ago, and they're not releasing her for at least another two days. They've been pumping her full of antibiotics since they admitted her."

"Jesus!" Gabe nearly shouted. "Why the hell didn't you or Lacey tell me?"

"Why would we? You broke up with her and haven't spoken to her in weeks," Peter said.

Gabe dug into his pocket and pulled out his truck keys as Peter frowned at him. "Where are you going?"

"To the hospital," Gabe said.

"I don't think that's a good idea," Peter said. "Lacey is with her, and Morgan is doing better. I'll have your sister talk to her, and if she wants to see you, we'll let you know."

"I'm going, Peter," Gabe growled, pushing past the man. He climbed into his truck and drove away, trying to ignore the panic that had engulfed him.

* * *

"She's sleeping, Gabe." Lacey was waiting for him, and she blocked the doorway to the hospital room. Gabe picked her up around the waist and moved her aside without speaking.

She huffed with annoyance as he strode into the room. It was a semi-private room with an older woman lying in the first bed. She gave him a cool, assessing look as he passed her and peeked around the curtain drawn around the second bed.

Morgan lay in the hospital bed. Her face was pale and thinner, but he still felt a rush of relief at seeing her sweet face. He sat in the chair beside the bed and picked up her hand.

"Don't wake her – she needs rest." Lacey hurried in after him.

"You should have told me, Lacey." He brushed a stray strand of hair back from Morgan's face and let his fingers linger on her soft cheek.

"She asked me not to. You hurt her badly, Gabriel."

"I know," he said.

Lacey rested her hand on his shoulder. "You've seen her. You should go now."

"No."

"Gabe -"

"I'm not leaving her. If you want me to leave, you'll have to bring security in and trust me, I'll make a scene."

She snorted in anger. "Gabriel Dern, you are the most stubborn man alive."

"How bad is it?" he asked.

"It could have been much worse. She was feeling shaky and nauseous at work. She had a high temperature, and the nurse at the school asked the administrators to call an ambulance for her. She got lucky. It wasn't severe sepsis, and it didn't damage any of her internal organs, but they decided to keep her at the hospital for a few days so they could monitor her while they gave her IV antibiotics. Plus, the cut on her leg was pretty bad. The doctor had to make the cut longer and deeper to drain the pus and infection from it, and for the first few days, it had a drain in it. The drain is out now, and they stitched the cut, but it's pretty sore."

"You should have called me." He could hear the anger in his voice.

She scowled at him. "I told you before – she asked me not to."

He didn't reply, and she sighed and kissed his head. "Tell Morgan that Nat spilled the beans, not me. And tell her I'll see her tomorrow."

"I will." Gabe continued to stroke Morgan's face.

"Gabe?"

"Yeah?"

"I love you."

"I love you too."

* * *

"I'm sorry, sir, visiting hours are over. You'll have to come back in the morning." The nurse tapped him on the shoulder.

"I'd like to stay the night."

"Only family members are allowed to stay after visiting hours," the nurse said.

"I'm her boyfriend." Gabe smiled at her.

"Really?" The nurse gave him a suspicious look. "She's been here nearly a week, and you're just showing up now?"

"I was out of the country. It took me a few days to get back."

The nurse sighed. "Sir, I think -"

"Are you Gabe then?" The older woman in the bed beside Morgan had poked her head around the curtain.

"Yes."

The woman looked at the nurse. "He's her boyfriend. She talks about him enough."

The nurse pursed her lips before shrugging. "Fine, you're allowed to stay. I need to change the bandage on her leg. Can you step back, please?"

Gabe nodded and moved out of the way as the nurse pulled the sheets down. Morgan's right leg was bandaged from her knee to nearly the top of her thigh, and he sucked in his breath when the nurse unwrapped the bandage.

"Jesus Christ," he whispered.

He stared at the long cut that snaked down her thigh and stopped above her knee. Although it was healing, the skin around the stitches was swollen and sore looking.

"Is it strange that she hasn't woken up at all?" Gabe asked worriedly. He had been there for nearly three hours, and she hadn't stirred.

The nurse shook her head as she finished wrapping Morgan's leg. "No. She was awake for most of the day, and the pain medication we give her makes her sleepy. She'll probably sleep through the night, so you might as well go home and get some rest."

"I'd rather stay." Gabe sat back down and picked up Morgan's hand as the nurse left the room.

The older woman poked her head around the curtain again.

"Thanks." Gabe gave her a small smile as she let her eyes drift over his ruined face.

"Ayuh. How did you get those scars?" she asked.

"I was in a car accident. The car caught on fire." Most people didn't mention his scars, and the woman's bluntness surprised him enough to answer.

"I'm sorry to hear that." She squinted at him. "You're a good looking fella, aren't you? Even with those scars. I can see why she fancies you."

Blushing a little, Gabe stared at the woman. "Does she really talk about me?"

"Ayuh, she does. O'course, she only says your name when she's sleeping, but it's still talking about you, ain't it?"

"Yeah, I guess it is."

"Are you her boyfriend?"

"I used to be, sort of."

"Well, used-to-be-her-boyfriend Gabe, my name is Mary."

"Hello, Mary."

The old woman dragged a chair over and sat on the other side of Morgan's bed. She patted Morgan's arm gently. "She's a sweet girl then, ain't she?"

Gabe nodded. "Yes, she's very sweet."

"Did you mess it up, or did she?"

"I did."

"Ayuh, I figured. Not to be sexist, sort-of-her-boyfriend Gabe, but it's been my experience that it's usually the fella who messes it up. If you don't mind me askin', what did you do?"

"I told her I wasn't good enough for her and didn't want to see her anymore."

"Not good for her? Why is that?" Mary asked.

Gabe laughed bitterly. "Look at me and look at her."

Mary stared at him for a long moment, her eyes roaming over the scars on his face. "All I see is a man in love."

"She deserves to be with someone who looks normal."

Mary snorted. "Normal? What's normal these days? I have a grandson who puts things in his ears that stretch his lobes out. Why, I could fit a damn marker through the holes in his lobes. My granddaughter has tattoos covering both arms from shoulder to wrists. Sleeves, she calls them. Says it's all the rage now, and they make her look cool."

She snorted again. "I say they make her look like a biker's whore, but I'm an old woman. What do I know about cool?"

Gabe blinked at her in surprise and startled himself and Mary by laughing loudly.

Mary grinned at him. "I ain't told her, but I've been considering getting a tattoo. Always thought a flower tattoo on my arm would be pretty. A rose or maybe a daisy. What do you think?"

"I think if you want a tattoo, you should get one," Gabe said.

"How long have you been all scarred up, maybe-you're-her-boyfriend-and-maybe-you're-not Gabe?"

"Since I was a teenager, ma'am."

"She the first woman to see past the scars?"

Gabe nodded and lifted Morgan's hand to his mouth. He kissed each knuckle gently before returning it to the bed.

"Ayuh, I ain't surprised. Did I mention that she was a sweet girl?"

"Yes."

"Cursed something awful when she first came in, though. She was determined she wasn't going to stay. I think the fever was making her a bit delirious."

Gabe smiled a little. "She doesn't normally curse."

"So if she don't see the scars, then what's the problem?"

He sighed. "Morgan is a gorgeous woman. She's outgoing and social, and I barely leave my house. People – people talk about me. I'm the town freak, and Morgan feels the need to defend me. How long will it take before she grows tired of defending me? Before she tires of listening to the whispers and seeing the stares when we walk down the street together?"

"Does she love you?"

"I don't know. She might have once, maybe, but I hurt her badly. I told her I was using her. She moved out, and now I don't even know where she's living." Gabe stared down at his hands. He had no idea why he was spilling his guts to the older woman, but it felt good to confide in her.

"I don't want to ruin her life like mine," he said.

"Ruin her life? Why? Because she happened to fall in love with a man who ain't got the face of a model?"

He gave her a dry look. "It's more than just not looking like a model, Mary."

"Good Lord, boy. I swear I ain't ever met a man as vain as you. So what if you ain't conventionally pretty? Looks aren't everything. I don't know Morgan well, but she doesn't seem like the kind of girl wrapped up in what her man looks like."

"I told you, it isn't about that. It's about her having to live her life constantly defending me or listening to people talk about how she's with the town freak," Gabe said.

Mary shrugged. "According to his math teacher, my grandson holds the title of town freak. It ain't nothin' but a simple matter of perception, Gabe. You think you're the town freak because you want to think that."

Gabe glared at her. "You think I want to have people staring at me? Whispering behind my back?"

"I never said that," Mary said. "I'll ask you not to put words in my mouth."

"Sorry, ma'am," Gabe muttered.

Mary heaved herself to her feet, wincing a little and rubbing at her side before she reached across the bed and patted Gabe's shoulder. "I know I'm being nothing but a nosy old biddy, and I'll leave you to your woman now. But before I go, would you take some advice from an old woman who has lived long enough to gain some wisdom?"

"Yes, ma'am."

"Let your woman decide what's best for her life. I know you love her and want to protect her, but she's a grown woman. If she wants to spend her life with you, you need to celebrate that, not push her away."

Gabe stared at the bed as Mary squeezed his shoulder. "Good night, Gabe."

"Good night, Mary. Thank you."

"Ayuh." She pushed past the curtain, and he heard her grunting softly as she climbed into bed.

He hesitated and then leaned down and kissed Morgan's mouth. She didn't stir, and he sat back and closed his eyes, keeping her hand clasped loosely in his.

CHAPTER 16

"Why are you here?"

Gabe jerked in the chair and opened his eyes. He must have dozed off. He rubbed at the kink in his neck. He was dreaming about Morgan. He glanced at his watch. It was three in the morning, and –

"Why are you here, Gabe?"

He jerked again and looked at the bed. Morgan was awake and staring at him. He scooted closer and took her hand in his. "Hi. How are you feeling?"

She pulled her hand free and tucked it under the sheets. "I'm fine. Why are you here? I told Lacey not to tell you I was in the hospital."

"She didn't. Nat told me by accident." He cleared his throat. "I was worried about you."

She sighed and moved restlessly on the bed. "What time is it?"

"Just after three."

She squinted at him. "I'm pretty sure visiting hours are over."

"I told them I was your boyfriend, so they would let me stay." He gave her a small grin that she didn't return.

"Why would you do that?"

"I told you – I was worried about you. Peter said you had a bad blood infection."

"Well, you've seen me, and I'm doing fine. You should go home and get some sleep."

"Why didn't you go to the hospital?" he asked.

She sighed. "I get hurt all the time, Gabriel. I didn't expect it to get infected like that."

"You should have gone to the doctor, Morgan."

She glared at him. "Don't you dare lecture me, Mr. 'My appendix nearly exploded because I was too stubborn to go to the hospital' Dern. You have no right to badger me about not going to the hospital."

"You're right. I'm sorry," he said.

She muttered something under her breath that he couldn't hear, then threw back the covers.

"Where are you going?"

"I have to go to the bathroom," she snapped.

"Maybe you should call the nurse," he suggested.

"No. I can do it myself."

He hovered over her as she swung her legs over the side of the bed. She sat there momentarily, and he touched her back gently.

"Morgan, maybe you should -"

"I'm fine," she muttered. "Just help me stand up."

He hooked his hands in her armpits and lifted her to her feet. She balanced on her good leg for a moment before gingerly putting weight on her injured one. She flinched, her face losing what little colour it had, and he immediately scooped her up into his arms.

"Put me down."

"No. Hold onto the IV pole." He brushed past the curtain and carried her into the bathroom as she held the IV pole and pulled it behind them. He flicked the light on with his elbow before setting her down in front of the toilet.

"Go ahead. I'll wait."

She gave him a dirty look. "Out, Gabe. I'm not peeing in front of you."

He rolled his eyes. "It's no big deal. Just go, and then I'll carry you back to bed."

"No," she said. "Stand outside the door, and I'll let you know when I'm done."

He sighed but did as she asked. After about five minutes, she called his name, and he opened the door. She was standing next to the sink, her face white with little beads of sweat running down it, and he gave her a worried look before picking her up gingerly.

"Are you okay, honey?"

She nodded, her lips pressed together in a grim line. "Yeah, it's just sore."

She wrapped her fingers around the IV pole again, and he carried her back to the bed. Mary was curled into a little ball in the middle of her bed, and despite the rattling of the IV as it dragged behind them, she didn't stir. He sat Morgan carefully on the edge of the bed and then helped her swing her legs up before covering her with the sheet. She closed her eyes and sighed deeply.

Frowning, he pushed the call button for the nurse. A few minutes later, she peered around the curtain.

"What's wrong?"

"She's in a lot of pain and feels warm," Gabe said.

The nurse took her wrist and counted her pulse before brushing her hand across her forehead. "How are you feeling, Morgan?"

"I'm fine, thanks, Leanne. I don't have a fever. I'm just tired," Morgan said as the nurse stuck a thermometer in her ear.

"Your temp is good." Leanne smiled at Morgan. "Lots of pain right now?"

"A little. I had to use the bathroom."

"Did you walk on your leg?" Leanne frowned.

Morgan shook her head. "No, Gabe carried me."

"Good. We'll get you up on some crutches tomorrow, but stay off the leg for now, okay?" She checked her watch. "You're due for some more pain meds anyway. I'll be right back."

She ducked out from the curtain, and Gabe followed her. "Is it normal for her to be this tired and in so much pain?"

Leanne nodded. "Yes. She'll be tired for a few more days, and the cut on her leg was badly infected, so it's not surprising it's painful. Give her another week, and she'll be back to her old self."

She left the room, and Gabe returned to Morgan, and picked up her hand.

"Why are you still here?" She squinted at him.

"If you want me to leave, I will, honey."

When she didn't answer, he squeezed her hand. "Honey, do you want me to go?"

"No," she said grudgingly before closing her eyes. "But stop calling me honey."

"Okay, sweetheart."

The corners of her mouth turned up slightly before she pressed her lips together and turned her face away from him. He breathed a sigh of relief. Maybe she didn't completely hate him after all.

* * *

"WHAT THE HELL?" GABE STARED IN CONFUSION AT THE EMPTY hospital bed before turning to Mary. "When did she get discharged?"

"About half an hour ago."

He cursed and hit his thigh in frustration. "She told me she wasn't being discharged until this afternoon."

After spending the night with Morgan, he'd needed to return home to finish a client's work project. It had taken him most of the day, but he'd assumed Morgan would let him spend the night, so he hadn't been too upset about missing the day with her. He'd shown up half an hour before visiting hours were over and protested vehemently when Morgan insisted he return home to sleep in his own bed. She refused to be swayed, and he had no choice but to leave.

He'd shown up as soon as visiting hours started this morning, determined to be there when she was discharged so that he could be the one to take her home.

"I guess they decided to discharge her early," Mary said.

"How did she get home?"

Lacey and Peter were at work, and she couldn't drive herself. Her leg was better, but she was using crutches to get around.

"She said a friend was picking her up," Mary said.

"What friend? She should have called me." He heard the poutiness in his voice and flushed a little. Why would Morgan call him? Maybe she didn't hate his guts, but he had broken her heart. Still, he couldn't stand the thought of her being alone. Unfortunately, he had no idea where Morgan lived and he had already badgered Lacey enough times about it to know she wouldn't tell him.

"Son of a bitch," he grunted and started toward the door of the room.

"You know how sweet that woman of yours is?" Mary asked him as he passed by her bed.

He blew his breath out in a frustrated rush. "How sweet?"

"She told me that as soon as I got out of this blasted hospital bed, she and I were going to have coffee."

"That's nice, Mary. I'm sorry, but I should get going." Maybe he could try bugging Lacey again.

"Oh, of course, of course. You young people are always in a hurry," Mary said. "Why, Morgan even gave me her phone number and address so I could visit her place. She wrote it down right here on this piece of paper."

He whipped around and stared at Mary. She held a piece of paper in her hand and grinned at him. "Your woman has lovely handwriting. Probably because she's a teacher."

"Probably," he said hoarsely. He took a few steps towards the bed. "Mary, would you mind if I -"

"Hush up for a minute, son." She held the piece of paper on her lap. "I'll give you the address, but you have to make me a promise."

"What's the promise?" he asked.

"You need to promise me you'll do everything possible to win her heart back. She loves you something fierce. She won't admit it, but I've spent nearly a week sharing this damn room with her, and I know a woman in love when I see one. I know she's angry with you and has every right to be, but I believe she'll forgive you if you straighten up and do what's right."

"I promise." He reached for the paper, and she slapped him lightly on the hand.

"Do you know the right thing to do, sort-of-her-boyfriend Gabe?"

"Yes, ma'am, I do."

She stared shrewdly at him for a moment before handing him the paper. "Yes, I believe you do."

He scanned the address and then gave it back to her. "Thank you, Mary. I owe you one."

She laughed. "Yes, I reckon you do." She pointed to her cheek, and he bent and kissed her wrinkled skin.

She grinned at him like a girl. "Now we're even. Good luck, Gabe."

"Thank you, Mary."

CHAPTER 17

Morgan stood in the lobby of her building and stared glumly at the stairs. She really hadn't thought this through when she'd taken an Uber home instead of calling Lacey. Her apartment was only on the third floor, but the building was old, and the elevator had been broken the entire two months she'd lived here. She gave the elevator a hopeful glance, praying they had fixed it while she was in the hospital, but the same "out of order" sign was still taped to its doors.

"Son of a biscuit." She'd been standing in the lobby for nearly fifteen minutes, weighing her options, and her leg was throbbing. She hooked her overnight bag across her body, tucked her crutches under her arms, and thumped her way to the bottom of the stairs.

She turned around and, with a small grimace of distaste at the filthy carpet she was about to sit on, placed the crutches on the stairs and lowered herself carefully onto the third stair. She scooted her butt up a stair. Her overnight bag pulled at her throat, and she carefully adjusted it before lifting herself to the next step.

"Only thirty-two more to go," she said.

The lobby door opened, the security lock worked about as well as the elevators did, and Gabe swept in. He glanced anxiously around the lobby before his gaze fell on her.

"Morgan! What the hell are you doing?" He ran forward and put his hand on her good leg.

"What does it look like I'm doing?" She said crossly. "I'm going up the stairs."

He glanced at the out-of-order sign on the elevator before bending over her. "Let me help you."

"I don't need your help. I'm perfectly fine."

He stuck one arm under her legs and his other around her back and lifted her easily. He started up the stairs, and she shoved at his shoulder. "My crutches!"

He bent, and she picked them up as he climbed to the first landing. "What floor are you on?" he puffed.

"The third," she said sweetly.

"Christ," he muttered but gamely carried on.

"How do you know where I live?" She frowned at him as he climbed the stairs. "Did your sister tell you? Because I specifically told her not to."

"Mary gave me your address," he panted.

"Why that sneaky old woman - I thought she had my back," Morgan said without much rancor.

He climbed steadily up the second set of stairs. "It's a good job she gave it to me. It would have taken you hours to get up these damn stairs."

"It would not have," she said indignantly as she opened the stairwell door for them. "I had it all under control."

"Of course you did," he grunted as he carried her to her apartment door and set her down in front of it.

She pulled her key out of her bag and opened it. Before she could tuck her crutches under her arms, Gabe picked her up again and carried her into the apartment.

He glanced around at the small room, his eyes narrowing with anger. "You are not staying here, Morgan."

"What are you talking about? It's perfectly fine."

"Like hell it is."

The apartment was a small bachelor suite. The ceiling was covered in water stains, and the walls were painted a dingy grey. The appliances were old, and she had barely any furniture. He stared with distaste at the mattress on the floor.

"Where's your furniture?"

"I haven't bought any yet. The guesthouse at the farm was furnished, so I didn't need any when I lived there. I'm not planning on staying here for long, so there's no point in buying furniture."

"Why are you even staying in this godforsaken place anyway?" He frowned.

She rolled her eyes. "It's not that bad. Stop being so dramatic. You have no idea how difficult it is on a teacher's salary to find a nice townhouse or condo to buy in this town. I lived in a motel for two months before Lacey offered me the guesthouse. I didn't want to stay in a motel again, so I rented something cheap until I find a place to buy that fits my budget."

She tugged at his arm. "You can put me down now, Gabriel."

He shook his head. "I'm serious, Morgan. You're not staying here. It isn't safe."

"Oh, for goodness sake! It's fine."

"The door to the lobby has no lock, the lock on your apartment door is flimsy as hell, and what if there was a fire? How would you leave the building with your leg like that?"

He set her on her feet and walked to where the mattress lay on the floor. She had no dresser, and her clothes were stacked neatly in her suitcase. He checked out the door on

the far right and grunted with satisfaction before disappearing into the bathroom. He reappeared with her toiletry
bag in his hand.

Balancing in the middle of the room on her one good leg,
Morgan watched as Gabe dropped her bag of toiletries into
the suitcase and then closed and zipped the suitcase. "What
are you doing?"

"Packing your things."

"Just where the heck am I supposed to go, Gabe? This
place may not be much, but it's my home, and I don't appreciate you -"

"You're coming back to the farmhouse." He carried her
suitcase to the door and set it down neatly.

She gaped at him in astonishment. "Oh no I am not,
Gabriel Dern."

"Yes, you are. No arguments."

"No arguments?" She crossed her arms over her chest.
"When exactly did you become my boss?"

"You took care of me when I came home from the hospital. Now it's my turn." He smiled at her.

She shook her head. "It doesn't work that way. I don't
need your help, and you made it clear that you don't want my
company."

His face fell, and he momentarily looked at the floor
before staring at her. "Morgan, please. I want to take care of
you and worry about you staying here alone. You'll need
some help for the next few days. You know you will. Please,
let me help you."

She sighed. "Gabe, I…"

"Just for the weekend. I'll bring you back here on Sunday
night, I promise."

She bit at her bottom lip. "Okay. But you should know
upfront that I'm not interested in being your friend or – or
anything else anymore. And this weekend isn't going to

change that."

"I know." He picked up her suitcase. "I'll be right back for you."

She nodded and watched him leave the apartment before rubbing her forehead. "This is a very bad idea, Morgan."

She sighed. It was only a bad idea because she was in love with Gabriel Dern, and two months apart from him had done nothing to change that love. While her leg was hurting, and she didn't relish the idea of staying in her crappy apartment all by herself, neither was the reason she had accepted his offer for help.

She missed Gabe with every fibre of her being and wondered if he could see through her flimsy excuses. She sighed again and stared moodily out the window. She would be wise to remember that Gabe may care about her, but nothing else had changed. He would never accept that they could have a relationship.

* * *

"This isn't a good idea, Morgan."

"It is," she insisted. "Please, Gabe. I really want to see Daisy and Lemon. I've missed them."

He sighed as he stacked the lunch dishes in the sink. "How does your leg feel today?"

"Fine. Much better than it was even yesterday."

He eyed her suspiciously as Morgan smiled hopefully at him. He brought her to the farmhouse yesterday and set her up in the guestroom. She spent most of the last twenty-four hours tucked into the bed. He brought her books to read and his laptop to surf the internet. She slept a lot the first day. She hadn't slept well in the hospital, and catching up on her sleep had gone a long way toward making her feel better.

"If I don't get fresh air and feel the sun on my face, I'll turn into a mushroom."

"Fine, but only on one condition."

"What?"

"You let me carry you to the barn."

"I have crutches."

"Don't take this wrong, but you can barely walk on two legs. I heard you fall last night when you got up to go to the bathroom."

"I didn't fall," she said. "I ran into the wall."

He didn't reply, so she crossed her arms over her chest and stared at the floor. She looked up in time to see the small grin cross his face.

"What are you smiling about?" she asked.

"You're adorable when you pout." He gave her another grin that made her heart speed up.

"I wasn't pouting. I was thinking." She ignored the way her heart was knocking against her ribcage and hoisted herself to her feet, using the table to steady herself. "Fine. You can carry me."

He picked her up, one arm curving around her waist and the other sliding under her legs as she put her arm tentatively around his broad shoulders. Immediately, a slow throbbing began in her lower body. She cursed to herself. Her nipples were tightening, and her cheeks were flushing, and she took a few deep breaths.

"Are you okay?" he asked as he walked out the door and down the porch steps.

Delilah and Vincent were dancing around his feet, and she frowned at him. "You're probably going to trip over those darn dogs and crush me under your body."

He laughed and tightened his hand around her ribs. "I promise if I start to fall, I'll toss you to safety."

She tamped down the giggle rising in her throat and

looked away from him. Her eyes lingered on his large hand. It was only inches from her breast, and she wanted to grab his hand and place it directly on her breast. Her nipples throbbed anew with the thought. They were visible through her t-shirt, and she had to fight the urge to cover them with her arm. Maybe he wouldn't notice.

She reached out and unlatched the barn door, and he pushed it open with his foot before carrying her inside. He set her down gently in front of Daisy's stall and steadied her with his hands on her upper arms. His gaze dropped to her breasts and lingered on the outline of her nipples against the fabric of her shirt.

His hands tightened on her arms, and he lifted his gaze to hers. Her breath squeaked out in a soft little moan at the look of dark need in his eyes.

"Gabe?" she said.

"Yeah?" He cupped her face, stroking her cheek with his thumb.

"Maybe you should get Lemon while I visit with Daisy."

He blinked at her and then nodded, disappointment carved into his face. She reached into the stall and petted Daisy's soft forehead as Gabe left the barn.

He returned after about ten minutes, his cheeks rosy from the chilly air, and picked her up without speaking. He and the dogs had herded the sheep toward their barn, and they were milling about in front of the large door that led to their pens. She searched the group for Lemon, her heart quickening when she saw her familiar, fuzzy body.

"Lemon," she called, but the ewe only stared at her.

"She's forgotten me," she said, feeling ridiculously sad.

"She hasn't. Just give her a minute," Gabe said.

"Lemon, come to Mama," she called.

She smiled happily when the ewe left the herd and trotted towards her. Lemon butted her head against her hip in a friendly manner, and Morgan petted and rubbed her soft head.

"She's getting so big." She smiled at Gabe.

"I think it's mostly wool," he laughed.

She petted and talked to the young ewe for nearly fifteen minutes. Gabe stood silently beside her before touching her arm. "You're starting to shiver, honey."

She nodded and leaned against the barn wall, watching as he opened the door of the sheep shed, and Vincent and Delilah herded the sheep into their pen. Lemon continued to stand beside her, and she petted the ewe one last time before pushing gently on her flank.

"Go on, Lemon."

The ewe took a few hesitant steps forward and ran into the shed when Vincent crowded behind her and nipped at her right leg. Gabe settled the sheep into their pen and returned to Morgan. He frowned at how she was shaking, picked her up, and carried her back to the farmhouse.

She stared over his shoulder at the guesthouse as he climbed the porch steps. Her heart ached at the sight of it, and a small sigh slipped from her throat. He squeezed her tightly.

"You okay?"

"Yeah. I miss it," she said.

"You could move back in," he said.

"That's not a good idea, Gabe. You know that."

He nodded and carried her into the house. She sighed with relief at the warmth. Her leg was aching from the cold, and she said, "Can you take me into the bathroom? I want to take a shower."

She hadn't had a shower since leaving the hospital yesterday morning, and she knew a hot shower would help warm her up and ease the throbbing in her leg.

He frowned but carried her to the bathroom. He set her

down next to the tub and said, "I'm afraid you'll fall in the shower."

"I won't." She bent and turned the shower on, testing the water with her hand. She adjusted the knobs until the water was steaming and turned to face him. "You can go now."

"Maybe I should stay and help you. You fall in the tub all the time."

She flushed bright red. "No way. You're not seeing me naked."

"I've already seen you naked," he pointed out.

"It's different now."

His brow creased, and she cut him off before he could begin to protest. "I'll be fine. If I need your help, I'll call for you, okay?"

He nodded. "I'll be right outside the bathroom door."

"Thank you."

She waited until he had closed the door before stripping off her shirt and bra. She wiggled awkwardly out of her pants and underwear, grunting irritably when her underwear tangled around her ankles.

"Morgan? Are you okay?" Gabe called through the door.

"Fine," she said as she pulled her panties from her feet.

Moving carefully, she sat on the side of the tub and lifted her legs into the tub. She pushed off, balancing carefully on her good leg and stood under the hot spray of water. It felt amazing, and she stood for long moments before, with a soft sigh, beginning to wash her hair.

CHAPTER 18

"Wake up, Gabe." Morgan shook Gabe as he moaned and cried out, his body twisting on the bed. "Wake up now. Come on, honey."

With a shuddering gasp, he tore himself out of the dream. He sat up in the bed, staring blankly at her as she patted his arm. "You're okay. It was just a nightmare."

Morgan's heart clenched painfully at Gabe's look of naked fear. She had woken in the night to hear him moaning and crying out. She lay in her bed staring at the ceiling for nearly five minutes before she climbed out, grabbed her crutches, and hobbled to his room.

"Morgan?" he rasped.

"Yeah. You're okay." She hesitated and then placed her hand on his bare chest and rubbed.

She didn't like how he looked – trembling and pale with tears glinting in his eyes. She continued to rub his chest, her fingers tracing the scarred skin, while he stared up at her. After a few moments, she smiled shakily at him and stood up.

"Don't leave me!" He grabbed her arm with panicky tightness, and she sat on the bed again.

She stroked his face, and he leaned into her hand. She wondered how often he had nightmares. They hadn't spent that many nights together, but he had slept peacefully each night she was with him.

"Honey, how often do you have nightmares?" she asked.

He looked out the window at the cold darkness. "Every night."

"I don't remember you having them when we were together."

"You kept them away."

Her heart broke a little, and she patted him on the shoulder. "Move over, honey."

He shifted over, and she pushed back the covers and slid in beside him. She flinched as she turned on her side but reached out and pulled on his shoulders. "Come here."

* * *

GABE HESITATED BEFORE PRESSING HIS BODY UP AGAINST Morgan's. He buried his face in her throat as she rubbed his back and breathed in her familiar scent.

The nightmare was particularly terrible tonight. He was back in the car, trapped in his seat with the flames licking closer and closer to him. He had looked for Tony in the driver's seat and was horrified to see Morgan sitting there instead. She was staring at him, her face full of pain and fear, and he renewed his struggles to free himself.

"Gabe," she whispered. "Please, help me."

He reached for her, his hand stretching out as the distance between their seats grew to an impossible length. The flames were touching her now, her clothes catching on fire and the skin on her face beginning to bubble and peel as the scorching heat engulfed them both.

He opened his mouth to scream when her voice had broken through the nightmare and pulled him out. Her voice and sweet face were a soothing balm to his soul, and he couldn't argue when she joined him in his bed.

He was trembling again, and she stroked his back before kissing him on the cheek. "You're okay, honey. Everything's okay."

"I'm so sorry," he rasped.

"For what?"

"I'm supposed to be taking care of you."

She squeezed him tightly. "Don't worry about it."

He leaned back a little and looked at her. "I miss you."

She bit her bottom lip and blinked rapidly before clearing her throat. "Go to sleep, Gabe."

"I'm so sorry I hurt you." He cupped her face and rested his forehead against hers. "I'm so sorry for everything."

"Gabe…"

He kissed her forehead and the tip of her nose when she said nothing else. "Say it, Morgan. Just tell me that you hate me now. You'll feel better."

"I don't hate you."

"You should," he whispered.

She stared at him. Their faces were very close now and he could feel her warm breath on his mouth. She took a shuddering breath, and then her mouth was on his, and she was kissing him with a deep and frantic need.

He groaned and returned her kiss before pulling away abruptly. "Morgan, wait. This isn't – I didn't mean for you to -"

"Kiss me, Gabe. I miss you too. Please, I miss you so much."

He lowered his mouth to hers, and they kissed with slow

and tender strokes of their lips and tongues. He cupped her breast through her t-shirt, teasing her nipple into a hard point as she arched her back and moaned.

"Naked," Morgan whispered. "I want you naked."

He yanked his boxers down his legs, kicking them off his feet impatiently, and then helped her shed her clothes. As he pulled her panties down her legs, he placed a gentle kiss on the bruised and stitched flesh of her leg.

"Honey, maybe we shouldn't do this. Your leg is -"

"No." She rose on her elbows, and he groaned at the sight of her breasts thrusting forward. "It's fine. We'll go slowly."

"Are you sure?" He placed a kiss on her knee, and she nodded.

"Very sure."

He gave her a searching look before kissing his way up her inner thigh. She spread her legs. He frowned at the way she winced, but she tugged on his hair, and he dipped his head and kissed the soft curls between her legs.

She sighed, and he licked her soft folds and warm flesh until she was soaking wet and moaning his name. He traced her swollen clit with the tip of his tongue, and she dug her nails into his scalp.

"Please, Gabe. I need you inside of me," she begged.

He kissed his way up her body and carefully positioned himself between her thighs. She wrapped her left leg around his hips, leaving her right one flat on the bed, and ran her fingers across his mouth.

"Tell me if I'm hurting you," he said.

"You won't." She reached between them and guided his cock into her tight opening. He groaned, and she made a soft noise of pleasure.

"It feels so good, Gabe. *You* feel so good," she said.

He moved in her with slow, controlled movements, and she arched her hips upward to meet each of his strokes.

He stared down at her and kissed her tenderly. He thrust back and forth before stopping with his cock buried deep inside of her. After a moment, she wiggled under him.

"Gabe, please." Although she knew he was moving slowly in deference to her injured thigh, his measured, unrelenting pace drove her mad with need. Having him stop completely was pure torture.

"I love you, Morgan."

She stiffened under him and looked at him with wide, shocked eyes.

"I love you," he repeated and moved in her with gentle, steady thrusts.

She was going to climax soon. She could feel it building in her belly and pelvis, and as the pleasure built to an almost unbearable level, she wrapped her arms around his shoulders and pressed her mouth to his ear. "I love you too, Gabe."

At her softly uttered words, he cried out and came deep within her. His climax triggered her own, and she shook and shuddered beneath him. Her thigh protested, but the pleasure overpowered the pain, and she arched her body into him and whispered she loved him again before collapsing on the bed.

He kissed her mouth, her cheeks, her throat and her upper chest before easing off of her and lying on his back beside her. He gathered her into his arms, pressing her head against his chest and rubbing her lower back.

* * *

"THIS WAS A MISTAKE."

They had been lying in the darkness for over an hour, and he thought she had fallen asleep.

He pulled her closer and pressed a kiss to her forehead. "It wasn't. Don't say that."

"It was," she insisted.

He sat up and reached for the bedside lamp. He turned to face her as the light illuminated the room with a soft glow.

"I love you, Morgan. It wasn't a mistake."

Her lips were trembling as she sat up. He reached for her, and she shied away from him. "Please don't, Gabe."

"Morgan -"

She started to cry, and he gave her a helpless look. "Please, honey. I'm sorry. I didn't mean to hurt you."

She swiped at the tears almost angrily. "I know. I want you to know that what I'm about to say doesn't change the fact that I love you, too, okay?"

He nodded and, unable to help himself, reached out and snagged her hand. She stared down at their clasped hands. "I've been thinking a lot for the last couple of months and realized that you're right. I've been in love with you for a while now, and at first, I thought it would be enough. That everything else didn't matter and just loving each other would be enough to make it work."

She raised her head and gave him a trembling smile. "Except I've realized that this isn't some fairy tale. It isn't a stupid Beauty and the Beast story where my loving you fixes your pain and gives us a happy ending."

She reached out and traced the scars on his face. "This is real life, and our problems can't be solved with a kiss and a declaration of love. No matter what I say or do or how much I love you, there will always be a part of you that thinks you're not good enough for me."

She sighed. "You're right, you know. I keep saying that it won't bother me if you want to keep cutting yourself off from the rest of the world, but the truth is, I don't know if it won't. I want to believe that it won't bother me. I want to be the person who understands your fears and accepts you for exactly who you are because you deserve that, Gabriel. You're a wonderful man, and I know you think you're not good enough for me, but honestly, I'm not sure I'm good enough for you."

"You are, Morgan," he said. "You're the sweetest, kindest person I know, and I love you."

She brushed at the tears spilling down her cheeks. "I'm worried that I'm not the person I think I am. That, five years down the road or two years or ten years, I start to resent you for not joining me at parties or weddings or even the grocery store. I'll break your heart."

"Morgan -"

She shook her head. "I can't stand the thought of hurting you like that, Gabe. I think it's better if we end this now before we start to love too deeply."

It's too late, he thought bleakly before he squeezed her hand.

"I'll try, Morgan. I'll make an effort to rejoin the world. I can't make any promises, but I'll do my best."

"No." She sniffed and wiped at her nose with the heel of her hand. "I won't ask you to do that. It isn't fair."

She stroked the side of his face again. "I know you want to try. I can't tell you how much I love you for that, but don't you see what will happen? You'll be miserable, and eventually, you'll resent me. Our love for each other will disappear under a cloud of anger and resentment."

She suddenly leaned forward and gave him a hard kiss before reaching for her t-shirt and slipping it over her head. "I should go back to my room."

"Stay the night with me, Morgan."

"I can't, honey. And I know I said I would stay until Sunday, but I think it's better if you take me home in the morning. I'll be fine, and I promise I'll text you if I need anything."

"So that's it? You're not even going to let me try? I'm just supposed to walk away from the woman I love?" he said.

"Yes," she said.

He glared at her. "What if I don't want to? What if I can't?"

"You told me this wouldn't work two months ago and asked me to leave. I did, even though it broke my heart. Now I'm asking you to do the same for me."

His anger deflated like a balloon, leaving him feeling cold, empty, and sick. He watched as she sat on the side of the bed and reached for her crutches. Without looking at him, she thumped out of the room, closing the door softly behind her.

* * *

"HEY, LOOK AT YOU! NO CRUTCHES!" LACEY GRINNED AT Morgan and pulled her into a brief, hard hug.

"Yup, and no stitches either. The doctor removed them today."

"That's wonderful!" Lacey said as Peter and Natalia joined them.

It had been a week since Gabe had driven her back to her apartment, carried her up the stairs, and given her a slow and thorough kiss before leaving her. She had wanted to cry but held the tears back fiercely. It didn't matter how much she loved him. She needed to let him go.

"Hi, Ms. Wilson."

"Hi, Natalia."

"When are you coming back to school? I miss you."

"As a matter of fact," Morgan lifted the little girl into her arms and kissed her smooth cheek, "I'll be back on Monday."

"Really?" Nat gave her a delighted grin, and Morgan nodded.

"Yes. My leg is much better now."

The little girl wiggled against her as she looked at her mom. "Mama, Jade and Chris are at the monkey bars. Can I join them?"

Lacey nodded as Morgan set Nat on the ground. "Yes, you may, but you have to stay on the playground equipment and not go anywhere else unless you tell me or Daddy first. Do you understand?"

"Yes, Mama." Natalia skipped to the playground equipment.

"I'm so glad you came tonight, Morgan," Lacey said.

"Well, it's not every day a town celebrates its Centennial," Morgan said. She glanced around the park, which was filled with people. It looked like the entire town was here, chatting amongst themselves as they waited for the fireworks to begin. "What time do the fireworks start?"

"In about half an hour." Peter glanced at the darkening sky. "They're just waiting for it to be dark."

He glanced over at the monkey bars. "Nat! Be careful, honey." He wandered away to the playground equipment as Lacey turned to Morgan.

"How are you doing, honey?" she asked.

"Fine," Morgan lied. She bit her tongue to stop from asking about Gabe. He had texted her a couple of times to ask her how she was feeling and if she needed anything, but other than that, she hadn't spoken to him at all.

It's for the best, she reminded herself. She ignored Lacey's look of sympathy and sipped at her hot chocolate.

* * *

GABE PACED RESTLESSLY IN THE KITCHEN. VINCENT TRAILED after him, whining softly, and Gabe stopped to pet him. It was Saturday night, and even after nearly two and a half months, it still didn't feel right that Morgan wasn't here with him. He should be making her dinner while she did her laundry and, with nothing more than her low voice and soft laugh, filled the house with warmth and love.

He stared out the window into the growing darkness. She would be at the park tonight. She and the rest of the town would gather to celebrate the Centennial. Lacey had invited him and had even mentioned that she thought Morgan would be there, but he hadn't accepted her invitation.

Morgan loved him, but just as he had realized he would do anything to be with her, even trying to stop hiding away, she had changed her mind. He laughed bitterly. It served him right for breaking her heart the way he had.

She needed to be with someone normal, someone who –

We had a deal, you and me, didn't we?

Mary's voice spoke dryly in his head, and for a moment, he was so sure the older woman was behind him that he spun around.

Only Vincent and Delilah stared back at him, and he rubbed his hand across his forehead. Mary's voice in his head may have been a figment of his imagination, but her words weren't. They had made a deal. Morgan's address in exchange for doing the right thing.

I tried, he thought. *I tried, and she rejected me.*

You didn't try hard enough, Mary said.

He swore softly. Mary was right. He hadn't tried hard enough. He loved Morgan, and the thought of spending the rest of his life without her was terrifying. He grabbed his jacket and shrugged into it. He would find Morgan and make her understand they were meant to be together, even if he had to do it in front of the whole damn town.

* * *

Peter, Natalia in his arms, joined Lacey and Morgan. "I think the fireworks are about to start."

Morgan glanced up at the sky. The stars were out and shining brightly, and she wrapped her arms around herself and took a deep breath. She would stop thinking about Gabe, stop wondering if he –

"Uncle Gabe!" Nat's delighted shout broke through her thoughts, and she stared bewildered at the little girl. Nat stared over Morgan's shoulder, and her heart beating wildly, Morgan whirled around.

Gabe strode toward them, his face grim and his shoulders set. If the others were staring at him, she didn't notice. The enormity of what he was doing, the gesture of love he displayed in seeking her out in a park filled with people, had brought on a surge of such overwhelming love and pride for him that she thought she might faint.

Watching him have the courage to come to the park, even knowing that most of the town would be there, she instantly realized she had been wrong. Gabe loved her and was willing to face his fears and be with her. She needed to give their love a chance. Nothing else mattered but being with him.

She staggered forward on trembling legs, not resisting when he reached out and pulled her into his arms. He kissed her, his hand tangling in her hair and his arm sliding around her waist.

"I love you, Morgan. I know you don't think we can make it work, but you're wrong. I'll do whatever it takes to make you happy, and I promise I won't resent you for it. Give me a chance to prove that to you. I'll never -"

"Hush, honey," she said.

He stopped talking, and she cupped his face. "You're right. I was wrong. I can't live without you, and I don't care if we spend the rest of our lives never leaving the farmhouse. I need you. I love you."

He kissed her again, lifting her and pressing her trembling body against his. She kissed his scarred face as the fireworks exploded in the sky in brilliant blue and green streaks.

"Finally," Lacey said happily. "I thought the two of you would be miserable forever."

Gabe set Morgan down, and she took his hand and led him to his family. He stood behind her and wrapped his arms around her waist, pulling her back against his chest and resting his chin on her head.

They watched the fireworks light up the night sky. When she squeezed his arms, he bent down, and she said, "I'm looking for a place to rent. I heard you have a pretty nice carriage house."

"Actually," he said solemnly, "the carriage house is no longer available."

She frowned at him, and he gave her a quick kiss. "But, I do have a room at the farmhouse. If you don't mind sharing a bed with a stubborn, idiotic sheep farmer."

She giggled. "Lucky for you, I prefer stubborn, idiotic sheep farmers."

He grinned and pulled her close. "I love you, Morgan Wilson."

"I love you too, Gabriel Dern."

Keep reading for an excerpt from Elizabeth Kelly's small town romance, "Sweet Harmony".

SWEET HARMONY EXCERPT

When the doorbell rang, Kira smoothed down her blonde hair and checked her reflection in the toaster. Not that it mattered what she looked like. This wasn't a first date, for God's sake.

She headed out of the kitchen and down the hallway. Two long windows flanked the front door, and she could see one tanned arm and hand through the right one. Her dentist had big hands.

You know what they say about big hands.

She flushed and tossed that errant thought out of her head before opening the door. She smiled at the dark-haired man standing on her front porch.

"Hello, Dr. MacMillan."

"Hello, Ms. Walker," he said.

There was a moment of awkward silence, and then she stepped back. "Call me Kira. Please, come in."

He stepped into the house, and she shut the door before squeezing past him. "Would you like something to drink? I have water, iced tea and soda. Or I can make coffee."

"An iced tea would be fine," he said.

As he followed her toward the kitchen, she wondered if he was checking out her ass in her yoga pants. She knew she didn't have a great body. She was on the thin side, and she secretly coveted Grace's full curves. She scoffed inwardly. Who was she kidding? Forget Grace's curves, she'd take Addison's very respectable C-cup boobs if given the chance. She was barely a B-cup, and her cleavage was thanks to the miracle invention of the century – the push-up bra.

Why she even thought her dentist would check out her ass was ridiculous. It was flat and –

Hey, Kira? Maybe you should stop thinking about your own damn tits and ass and get the man his iced tea.

Dr. MacMillan was hovering in the kitchen doorway while she stood blankly next to the fridge, and she gave him an embarrassed smile. "Sorry. Have a seat, and I'll get that iced tea."

"Thank you," he said.

She poured each of them a glass of iced tea and perched on the edge of the chair across from him. He drank some iced tea before saying, "It's good. Thanks."

"I like it a little on the sweet side," she said. "My brother says it's way too sweet and that I'll rot my teeth right out of my head, but I guess that's why I go to see you, right? To keep my teeth from rotting out of my head when I eat too much sweet stuff?"

Kira! Enough!

She shut her mouth with a snap. Fuck, what was wrong with her? Why was she so damn nervous? Sure, Dr. MacMillan was handsome enough, but he wasn't Daniel. She closed her eyes for a moment and conjured up an image of Daniel. It calmed her a little, and she took a deep breath. Daniel's blond hair and dark blue eyes were what she wanted.

Dr. MacMillan's eyes might be blue, but they were so

light they were almost transparent. She could see none of the warmth and humour in them that Daniel's gaze had. In fact, her dentist was currently staring at her like she was some new and interesting species of bug he had discovered crawling up his leg.

She cleared her throat. "Sorry, I babble when I'm nervous."

He took another drink of iced tea. "You have a nice home."

"Thank you. It was my childhood home. It belongs to my brother now, but he didn't want to live here. My parents died a few years ago, and being in the house brought on too many sad memories for him. I love living here, though. It makes me feel closer to my mom and dad, you know?"

She closed her mouth again. Holy shit, she was making the worst first impression ever.

"I'm sorry about your parents." His voice was a low rasp, and the sound of it sent the weirdest shiver down her spine.

"Thank you," she replied. "So, um, Grace said we could help each other with our problems."

He nodded. "Possibly."

She waited and tried not to sigh with frustration when he said nothing else. His silence was beginning to unnerve her. Daniel was chatty and always the life of the party. She could barely get a word in edgewise when she was with him, and she loved that. She loved his bold brashness and how he lit up a room when he walked into it.

Her dentist hardly made an impact. Hell, she'd met him how many times in his office, and she had no impression of him at all. He was just a masked guy who came in and checked her teeth at the end of the cleaning.

"So, you need a date for your cousin's wedding?" she asked.

"Yes," he said, "and you need a boyfriend to make Daniel Moore jealous."

His voice had the slightest hint of derision, and she immediately blushed. It was evident that he thought she was an idiot.

"You know what? Never mind, Dr. MacMillan." She stood and dumped her iced tea down the sink. "This isn't going to work. I'll show you out now."

She stalked toward the front door. She could hear him behind her, but before she could open the door, he wrapped his long fingers around her wrist. The touch of his skin against hers made another one of those little shivers zip down her spinal cord. She froze and turned to stare up at him.

"I'm sorry," he said. "I'm being an ass."

"Yes, you are."

He sighed and dropped her wrist before raking his hand through his dark hair. "I apologize. Also, if we're going to fake date, you should call me Connor."

"Why are you even here, Connor?" she asked. "It's obvious you think this is a stupid idea."

"It isn't," he said. "I'm just -"

He paused and rubbed at one temple. "What if this doesn't work?"

"What do you mean?"

"What if our fake dating doesn't make Daniel jealous? Will you still go with me to my cousin's wedding? Still pretend to be my girlfriend?"

"Yes," she said.

"What if it does work? Then what? You start dating Daniel, and I'm headed to Willington alone."

"Well, your cousin's wedding is in a month, right?"

"Yes."

"We don't have to start fake dating right away. We can

give it a couple of weeks and use that time to learn more about each other. It's probably a good idea if we know more than each other's names. It'll be more believable if we know personal stuff about each other. That leaves only two weeks until your cousin's wedding. I think it'll take more than a couple of weeks to make Daniel jealous," she said.

"Do I have your word that you'll attend the wedding with me?" he asked.

"Yes," she said. "I'll be there, no matter what."

Then we have an agreement," Connor said. "You'll pose as my girlfriend at my cousin's wedding, and I'll help you make Daniel seethe with jealousy and realize that you're his soul mate."

She gave him a dirty look. "You don't have to make it sound so juvenile."

He just shrugged, and she reached for the front door. "Thank you. I'll get your number from Grace and text you in the next few days about meeting to go over personal stuff."

"There's just one more thing," Connor said.

"What?"

"This." He gripped the back of her neck and pulled her forward. She made a decidedly stupid-sounding squeak when he bent his dark head and pressed his mouth against hers. She stood stock-still with her eyes wide and unblinking as he slid his other arm around her waist and pulled her against his hard body.

When he sucked on her lower lip, a strange tingle went through her lower body, and another small sound escaped her lips. This one, embarrassingly enough, sounded like a moan, and she tried to step back. His hand tightened around her neck, holding her completely immobile. When his tongue slid across her upper lip, she heard another of those odd moan-like noises as her eyes drifted shut.

God, he smells so good, she thought bewilderedly as he

tilted her head back. He kissed her again, his lips warm and weirdly persuasive, and it took her a minute to realize she was returning his kiss.

Kira! Stop kissing your dentist!

It was solid advice, but her body was completely and blissfully betraying her. She pressed up against Connor and put her arms around his neck. He was so tall that it was a real stretch to do it, but she liked the way it forced her breasts against his chest.

His tongue licked the seam of her mouth. Her head whirling and her pussy suddenly throbbing, she parted her lips. He slid his tongue between them and tasted her with slow, long licks that made Kira shudder with pleasure. He tasted sweet, like the iced tea he had been drinking. When she pushed her tongue into his mouth with a decided lack of finesse, he slid his fingers into her hair and tugged her back.

"Slow," he whispered.

She blushed fiercely. For roughly a nanosecond, she thought about telling him to stop, but then his warm mouth returned to hers, and he was urging her tongue back into his mouth with slow licks of his. She slowed down and mimicked the slow strokes of his tongue.

He groaned quietly. Besides his low whisper, it was the first sound he had made since kissing her. It flamed the lust in her belly even higher. She had a feeling that the icy Dr. Connor MacMillan never lost control. The idea that kissing her could make that control slip, even a little, was deliciously intoxicating.

She arched her back and rubbed her abdomen against the hardness pressing into it. Connor was hard. He was hard for her, and that sent another flickering flame of excitement through her nerve endings. She rubbed her small breasts against him and wondered what she could do to get him to touch them. Her nipples were almost painfully hard and poking against her bra. A sudden vision of Connor sucking on them brought on a gush of liquid that soaked the crotch of her panties.

He pulled away abruptly, and she would have fallen in a boneless heap to the floor if he hadn't steadied her. She stared dumbly at him before reaching up and touching her trembling, swollen lips.

"Why-why did you do that?" she whispered.

"If we're posing as boyfriend and girlfriend, it's going to require physical touching and kissing," he said.

She felt like she'd been through the wringer, but he wasn't even out of breath. If it hadn't been for the way his dick still strained at the front of his pants, she would have thought he was completely unaffected by the kiss between them.

"O-only when we're around other people." She couldn't seem to stop stuttering or touching her swollen mouth.

He gave her an impatient look. "It won't look very realistic if we kiss each other like it's the first time we've ever kissed. And I wanted to see if we had chemistry."

"Do we?" she asked like an idiot.

A brief smile crossed his face, sending a weird tingle down the base of her spine. "Yes. I think so, anyway."

She didn't reply, and he patted her shoulder like he was his sister. "That's a good thing, Kira. It will make it appear more real."

"Uh, right," she said.

He studied her. "How many men have you kissed before?"

"Why?"

"You're not," he paused, "great at kissing."

Her face was so red she was nearly sweating, and she gave him a furious look. "That's a really rude thing to say."

"No, just honest. We'll need to practice some more."

She wanted to tell him to take his idea of practice kissing and stuff it up his piehole, but strangely the thought of kissing him again wasn't entirely unpleasant. Besides, as much as it was a blow to her ego, he probably had a point. She'd kissed two men before him, and neither of them had provoked the type of reaction that her dentist's kiss did.

He opened the front door and asked, "What time do you work tomorrow?"

"Uh, I need to be at the office by nine."

"I'll stop by at eight, and we'll practice." He left, shutting the door quietly behind him, and she sank against the wall, her fingers still tracing her lower lip. What the hell just happened?

ABOUT THE AUTHOR

Elizabeth Kelly was born and raised in Ontario, Canada. She moved west as a teenager and now lives in Alberta with her husband and a menagerie of pets. She firmly believes that a person can survive solely on sushi and coffee, and only her husband's mad cooking skills prevents her from proving that theory.

For more information about Elizabeth, check out her website at

www.elizabethkelly.ca

- facebook.com/EKellyBooks
- x.com/ElizabethKBooks
- instagram.com/elizabethkelly_author
- amazon.com/Elizabeth-Kelly/e/B00EOHZ0MS
- bookbub.com/authors/elizabeth-kelly

ALSO BY ELIZABETH KELLY

Tempted Series

Tempted

Twice Tempted

Forever Tempted

Breathless

Tempted Trilogy (Books 1-3)

Red Moon Series

Red Moon

Red Moon Rising

Dark Moon

Alpha Moon

Pale Moon

The Recruit Series

The Recruit (Book One)

The Recruit (Book Two)

The Recruit (Book Three)

The Recruit (Book Four)

The Recruit (Book Five)

The Recruit (Book Six)

The Shifters Series

Willow and the Wolf (Book One)

Ava and the Bear (Book Two)

Katarina and the Bird (Book Three)

Porter's Mate (Book Four)

Bria and the Tiger (Book Five)

Rosalie Undone (Book Six)

The Dragon's Mate (Book Seven)

Rise of the Jaguar (Book Eight)

The Assassin and the Bear (Book Nine)

Elora and the Crow (Book Ten)

The Draax Series

Reign (Book One)

Rule (Book Two)

Rebel (Book Three)

Surrender (Book Four)

Survive (Book Five)

Salvation (Book Six)

Harmony Falls Series

Sweet Harmony (Book One)

Perfect Harmony (Book Two)

Forbidden Harmony (Book Three)

Redeeming Harmony (Book Four)

Absolute Harmony (Novella)

Beautiful Harmony (Book Five)

Reckless Harmony (Book Six)

Seasoned Romance Series

Bet Your Heart on Me (Book One)

Take a Chance on Me (Book Two)

Place Your Trust in Me (Book Three)

Individual Books

The Necessary Engagement

Amelia's Touch

The Rancher's Daughter

Healing Gabriel

The Contract

A Home for Lily

Saving Charlotte

Shameless

The Fairy Tales Collection

Broken

An Unlikely Seduction

Holiday Romance

The Christmas Wife

The Christmas Rescue

The Christmas Nanny

The Christmas Boss

Sordid Games

www.ingramcontent.com/pod-product-compliance
Lightning Source LLC
Chambersburg PA
CBHW060922180626
46817CB00004B/1353